A Voice
in Every Wind

Don Sakers

A VOICE IN EVERY WIND
copyright © 2003, Don Sakers

Published by
> Speed-of-C Productions
> PO Box 265
> Linthicum, MD 21090-0265

The stories in this book take place in The Scattered Worlds universe. In chronological sequence, it falls at 4.882. For more information, visit the Scattered Worlds website at *www.scatteredworlds.com*.

The first portion of this book appeared in *Amazing Stories*, January 1986.

ISBN: 978-1-934754-25- 2
Third edition June 2020

Dedication:

For unwavering friendship, shared joy, and mutual understanding of the creative temperament, *A Voice in Every Wind* is dedicated to Renfield and June.

Part One:

A Voice in Every Wind

A Voice in Every Wind

I have a copy of the Fifth Forbidden Book.

My friend Treyl was very anxious to see it; he did not realize that my people used books. So I led and Treyl followed with his strange ungainly waddle, away from the clevth and northward into the hills. This was in the time of the wet spring winds, when the rimmith bloom for their brief lives and the sun passes the Seam of Heaven in a shower of sparks. The clevth was upwind, and every gust brought the awareness of my people preparing for the time of breeding: young females ready to mate and drop their eggs in the shallows, half-year-olds anxious to pick up the beginnings of their coats, adolescents ready for a last taste of the ancestral waters before entering their final forms. The night was alive with sensation, alive in a way that made Treyl and the Fifth Forbidden Book so much more exciting.

With Treyl watching I carefully took the Book from its wrapping—cured membranes of the large jarief fish—and cradled it in my three forward hands. My copy of the Fifth Forbidden Book is a heavy thing, with leaves made from pressed plantfibers and separated by more membranes. As I held it, my hands detected its ancient holiness, and I caught a wisp of the long-ago scribe who had lovingly transferred the words of the original Book to this copy. I opened the Book to its first leaf, raised it to my face and caressed it with my antennae. Just as he had deposited them so long ago, I felt the thoughts of Ep-Naph the Great Warrior, thoughts that he had left to be preserved by the brotherhood for those of his descendants who could comprehend them.

Treyl leaned forward, looking naked without a coat of star-shaped pled by their hundreds, looking ready to fall over as he balanced on an amazing two limbs while reaching for me with the only other two he possessed. When I first met Treyl, I closed my mind against the onslaught of pain that had to emanate from one so crippled—only later I learned that his people are naturally malformed.

His backpack spoke: a combination of the soundless speech of my people, and the noisy chitters and clicks of the secret tongue of the brotherhood. "May I see it, Dleef?"

"It is old and fragile, my friend Treyl. Please take care as you would handling a newborn."

He left me holding the Book, removed an antenna from his backpack and brushed it lightly over the surface of the leaf. "Amazing. That chemical traces could be so exact. That your sensory apparatus can pick them up. That they convey so much information."

"The Book is old," I told him, "and was but a copy to begin with. Many passages have faded and are hard to read."

"My backpack can read them all. Possibly it can duplicate the chemicals and make those passages easier to read. Would you like me to do that?"

I regarded him well, this odd small creature from nowhere. The rest of the clevth bore him the usual disregard for a stranger who does not smell right; why did I trust him? Was it that other thing, which made me a part of the brotherhood and brought me the enmity of my people? Whatever, I knew that I *did* trust Treyl, trusted him with something in me that went beyond his smell and his strangeness. "The clevth leaves with morning, and although I do not wish to go south right now I shall accompany them. You may work your magics on the Book until daylight."

"Until daylight." He pressed one of his hands against mine, gently, to avoid hurting himself on my pled coat. And through the interstices and the living bodies of my pled seeped a measure of his alien feel, and once again I wondered about him.

About myself.

Treyl read, and the night deepened. The winds bore taste of my sleeping clevth, and of oh so much more: bands of hunting jrill on far-off plains, the scent of other clevths, and always the life-bearing fragrance of the sea.

The first of the great moons rose presently, its tiny half-disc swimming amid the glittery fish that live on the Seam of Heaven. Every night there is a gap in the Seam, a gap that slowly works its way from east to west—the brotherhood says it has been there since Ep-Naph died and shattered the world as it was. More is told of this in the Second Forbidden Book, which I have never seen.

Treyl says that the gap is the shadow of the world. The rest of my people do not think about it. Nor, most of the time, do I.

But there are times, times when a feeling comes that is at once different and familiar: when one looks at something one has known all her life, like the Gap or a rimmith blossom, like the summer winds or the tiny bodies and shells of one's own pled—and one begins to muse, to wonder.

It comes and it goes, this feeling, and even the brotherhood (the creator of speech) has no word for it. None is needed, for without the feeling there are no words; there is merely the language of the air and the land and the water, there is only the unknowing twitch of antennae, there is only snorting and growling and baying at the moons.

The night deepened, and in me that feeling ebbed.

The moon.

The taste of the clevth, and the far-off smell of hunting jrill.

The night winds caressed me, and I knew their messages without knowing, dozed without knowing I slept, awakened without awareness of what it means to wake. Most of my people live always this way, never tasting for a moment the terror and the joy of that feeling which the brotherhood does not name.

Treyl read.

When morning came, the Seam of Heaven announced the sun's arrival half a limb early, becoming a red arch across half the sky. And the winds told me that the clevth was awake, awake and ready to set out for the sea. Gone was all trace of my resolve to remain, to go north—now I responded by turning for the clevth and the sea.

Treyl wrapped the Fifth Forbidden Book, reverently, and without considering, I took it from his hands and tucked it under my pled coat in front, where the pled shells have grown and not anchored themselves to my thorax plate. I think Treyl's backpack spoke to me in the language of the brotherhood, but all I could hear was the voice of the winds, all I could do was answer them.

His backpack's long antenna touched me smelling of question, and I reassured him that all was right, that we were to join the clevth on its march south, that I knew of his presence and I approved.

Clevth.

Clevth is not a place, although place is important and the very soil of the clevth carries a part of its life and its memories. Clevth is people, yet people may leave and enter the clevth without altering its quality. Clevth is the animals that serve us and live with us, it is the houses in which we dwell and the spaces through which we move. Clevth is people, and it is much more: It is the smells, the feelings, the tastes of one's home. Clevth is a process, something always growing, always changing and never complete. The trace of all of us is in the clevth, and each adds to its structure.

For all that my clevth distrusts me and would at times have me gone, it is *my* clevth and it is what stands between me and...and something which I cannot name, but which I fear beyond terror.

*

That morning, with the sun mounting Heaven's Seam like a bead on a string, my clevth set out. Makers, farmers, herders; carriers, runners, shamans—all fell into their place, with their tools and their herds, with their burdens and rattles, with all the lesser beasts that accompany the clevth. And around them all, protecting, were the warriors. We are strong, and fast, and we have our own armor beneath our pled coats. And the greatest mystery of all, the brotherhood is made up only of warriors. The blood of Ep-Naph is ours, the heritage of Ep-Naph is ours, and if clevth exists at all it is because we defend it.

I stepped into my place, all about me the heady smells and tastes of the clevth on the move. Treyl walked hesitantly behind me, sandwiched between two young warriors who had only taken their forms last year.

That long march I spent much time pitying Treyl for his loneliness. At least when my spells struck I had Treyl to talk with, and I could hope to meet another of the brotherhood in my state, and I could dream that I would be normal once again. But Treyl had no normality, and he had no one to talk with but the voices from his backpack. So lonesome was the man, I imagined, that he believed those voices to come from the sky and to be talking to him alone. I felt then that they were nothing more than the random voices that one smells in the high cold winds atop the mountains, or in the currents of rivers that wash strange clevths.

For time and for time my clevth has moved south along the way, until the very rocks bear the smell of our passage. We merely follow, knowing that we will reach the breeding grounds before the females reach heat, the babies dry out, and the adolescents grow so large as to burst their skins.

Three days upon the march we came faces-to-faces and antennae-to-antennae with another clevth. This was in the rocky lowlands near the great river that bears the city Cora like an overripe fruit. Here the winds were strong from the left, blowing from out of the east with the scent of the sea.

The dance began. In meeting of clevths, always the dance is the master. We merely take our assigned positions, and allow the winds of the dance to move us.

The first movement belonged to us, the warriors. In the front lines we examined one another. The other clevth was mostly warriors; they had left all their other forms, but a few runners and shamans, at home. And they reeked of hostility.

Next movement belonged to the shamans. They took the front rank, and now messages flew back and forth with every gust and every touch: You do not belong here. Get out of our way. Go further and we will kill you. We will wipe you out to pass. The air grew absolutely thick with threats and counter-threats. The animals in our clevth set up fierce noises in response, and all other awareness faded beneath the overwhelming odor of hate.

This is the way of the dance.

And now the third movement began, the shamans retiring in good order as we warriors advanced. One last threat charged the air as before a summer storm—and then it broke. Without knowing what I did, I leaped. Another warrior tried to seize me, I danced backward, and he advanced with spears in his hands.

At once my stomach turned, and I was in my strange state. I saw Treyl behind me, fumbling at his backpack, and I felt the pressure of the Fifth Forbidden Book against my thorax plate.

And I remembered. The Fifth Forbidden Book is made up of Ep-Naph's words and thoughts about battles and military matters, about things that are the concern of warriors.

The wind gusted strong from the east. And now that I could remember—now that I could plan for the future—I recalled what Ep-Naph said: the upwind army usually wins.

Is there any reason, I asked myself, that we should always remain slaves of the dance? That we cannot act on our own? The clevth would never follow me—but it would follow the scent of success.

Now to succeed.

"Treyl. Help me. Get my clevth upwind of the others. There is no use being gentle, or trying to explain—just push them." For such a strange being, Treyl was stronger than he looked. He could shove an adult with little trouble. "Leave the warriors alone. Get the clevth upwind, and they will adjust their fighting naturally."

I ducked a foreign warrior's spear-cast. Easy to talk of moving my army upwind, difficult to do. For once the dance is joined and the lust of battle is upon a warrior, she has little else to do but fight, and go on fighting, until all the enemy are gone and their smell eradicated from the battlefield.

—That is why it works, Ep-Naph!! How clever you are, ancestor of mine. When the enemy-smell from my clevth drifts down among the others, they will become confused and may even battle one another. And we will win, though we have only half the warriors.

"Listen to me, my clevth!" With the language of my people, the language that is without words, I called to them. "Follow me, and the others will fall." Kevva, one of the young new warriors, was next to me. I touched her with two hands and let them carry the message—that the others would fall if we could move upwind and confuse them.

As the revelation had struck within my own self, I saw Kevva's eyes twitch with the realization of it. And Kevva moved to the left, going on to touch others around her.

Great Ep-Naph, not only did I have the power to speak with the brotherhood, to realize what the words of Ep-Naph meant...but I had the power to make others see as well.

For a moment I could feel the dance altering, and it was almost as if I held the dance between my hands, the way a maker holds a lump of clay he is molding.

Treyl was doing admirably, by the simple process of carrying youngsters and letting their distress-calls bring their elders. And Kevva and I in no time had a band of converted warriors following us. The direction of the dance itself was changing. The wind mounted, and I waded into the fighting, surrendering to the power of the dance.

By the time the sun had moved another limb up in the sky, we had won. The other clevth retreated, and cast forth the smell of defeat that calmed us and made us unable to follow. We re-grouped, then continued south.

I sought out Treyl, my elation swirling away with eddies of wind and dripping onto the rocks. "Treyl, did you see what happened? Did you see? It worked. My plan worked."

"I'm proud of you, Dleef. Yes, it worked. How did you manage to convince the others to go along with you? Your people are not much for original ideas, you know."

"I do not understand. Can your magic antenna tell us?"

Treyl whipped out the antenna, ran it over my body. He snorted as we walked. "A lot of unidentified enzymes being produced by your body, my friend." He paused, took out another, stiffer antenna, and stabbed it deeply into the body of one of the fallen warriors. The clevth marched on, ignoring him.

"Chance is going to have to analyze these data before he can come up with a hypothesis." Chance is the name Treyl gives to what he believes to be a large being like himself far up in the sky beyond the Seam of Heaven. To me, this sounded awfully like the nonsense of the shamans, and I supposed Treyl to be a kind of shaman himself.

"Then, we will let him."

Treyl plunged his stiff antenna into many other bodies, then brushed the battlefield in several places with other antennae. By this time the clevth was many steps away, and the two of us had to move very quickly to catch up.

We marched, Treyl muttered to his sky-voices, and I wondered at my new power.

*

Sea.

It makes itself known a day's march away. The power of the sea draws a clevth the way sweetfruit draws springflies. Our stretch of the sea is a sandy cove with gentle shallows which are strewn with reefs of pled. The sea smells and tastes like the naked blood that a warrior sheds for his clevth; it is soothing on the skin like nothing else.

Joy swept outward in crestless waves, as little ones and adults alike plunged into the surf. We warriors stood back, watching and ready to move, until the lazy taste of relaxation came to us off the sea-breeze, and we knew the clevth was safe. Then we splashed into the water. Within my coat and touching my flesh, I could feel the tiny pled rejoicing to be among their own kind.

Around me the maelstrom of breeding time began. It would be many days before it was all over, before the eggs were laid and cemented to their parents' coats, before the younglings emerged with the first of many pled clinging to them and starting to build the star-shaped shells that would eventually become a fine protective coat. For days and days they would lie thus, encased in a cocoon of pled shells, while inside a miraculous transformation built. Where adolescents had entered, out would come warriors, farmers, makers, and the other forms.

While breeding went on, I suddenly had one of my spells. Why should we have such ecstasy only when the sun felt like it? Why not take home some of these breeding waters in jars, and use them for the clevth? It was an idea that made me tremble, an idea that could almost have come from Treyl and his alienness.

Reminded, I looked for Treyl—found him sitting on the sand idly dragging his fingers to make patterns. Always it is hard to guess what Treyl is feeling, for the scents he gives off are odd and cryptic. Yet now I thought my friend was melancholy, and I reluctantly pulled myself from the water and crawled up the beach to sit next to him.

"Do your voices from the sky not speak with you?" I asked.

"They have nothing to say." He sighed, and my antennae twitched. Can it be that the scent of loneliness is the same for all people?

The sun was hot and dry, and all at once I thought that I must get into the water or I would parch right there. I left Treyl, and with the first gulp of breeding-water I forgot him, and spent the rest of my time wallowing with the others.

Days and days and days passed. Eggs stiffened and dried, until they could survive outside water. Younglings proudly showed off the marks where pled had attached to their skins. And then the breeding water took on a sharp acrid taste, and we all watched the hatching of adolescents into their new forms.

Treyl counted for me—thirty-two adolescents had entered cocoons. As I drew back from the water, I had a spell, and was able to keep track of the forms that emerged. Eight warriors, seven farmers, six makers and six herders, three carriers, and two runners. Treyl cocked his head, then his backpack spoke, translating his sounds into words.

"Running just along planetary averages," he said. I had the feeling he was talking to his sky-voices rather than to me. "Warriors are up twenty percent, while makers, farmers, and herders are down."

He didn't need to tell me this. The last few breeding cycles, the clevth has had more warriors than it needs. And not just our clevth, but every one we knew. The brotherhood says the problem includes even Metla and the Gelk lands.

"Why, Treyl? Why are more warriors being made?"

Treyl noticed me. "We're not sure. Something has upset the chemical balance of your clevths. A new enzyme is stirring around, changing the distribution of forms. We haven't been able to locate the center of its effect. At first it seemed to be Tar-Ve, then we followed the trail northward. Your clevth was a stop along the way."

Dripping, the new adults scuttled onto sand and presented themselves before our three shamans. The shamans twitched and touched, flicked antennae over the new ones. And the odor of dissatisfaction grew. Finally, inspection complete, the shamans turned to the clevth. All of us were massed on the beach, over three hundred adults with all the assorted dependents of the clevth. All waiting for judgement.

Our shamans seem to have a ritual dance for every occasion, and this was no exception. They jumped and flapped their limbs, moving through the clevth and touching everyone they could. Others joined the dance, and as a shaman passed upwind I sniffed a reproduction of my own scent. The dance began to circle about me, and in my hearts I felt dread. Treyl stood next to me, but the rest of the clevth withdrew to weave a pattern of accusation.

Yes, accusation. I heard Treyl's backpack whispering into his ears; I do not know how much of the display it understood. To me the meaning was clear. Too many warriors had formed, the shamans said. And I, Dleef the Mad, was held responsible. Shamans must blame something—for early snowfall that kills our crops, for awful sulfurous smells that waft in from the east and leave half the clevth disabled, for the formation of too many warriors at breeding time....

Now the scent of warriors entered the dance, that attack-scent which sooner or later is always mixed with the smell of death.

My death.

"Am I reading this aright?" Treyl asked.

I signaled assent. "My clevth wishes me dead."

"Because of me?"

"Because of what I am. Because I know the language of the brotherhood. Because I know you. Because they think my presence is causing more warriors to form."

"It *is*."

For a second I took my eyes off the clevth's dance of death. "You too, Treyl?"

Before he could answer, the dance broke and the nearest warriors rushed me. At their head was Kevva, lunging with claws extended and reeking of more murderous hate than a whole pack of hunting jrill.

A warrior is strong and fast. Each of us spends much time each day sharpening natural ridges in our pled coats, so that our arms are like knives, our back ridges like scrapers, the tips of our feet like spear heads. Kevva came at me now, as the others came behind her, brandishing those natural weapons with deadly skill.

One does not deliberate, one does not think—when attacked, one defends, defends to the limit of her ability. Kevva met my own sharp forearms; although I was braced with four legs her impact was jarring, and I felt my pled protesting and digging further into my skin with all their might. Kevva pulled back, pled coat over her chest cracked.

I drew my spear and lunged. The fracture in her coat was weak and it broke—I thrust with all my might as Kevva's blood splashed over me and over the ground. Then Kevva fell, my spear buried deep in her chest. In the blood that had touched me—as well as in her eyes—I thought I read her too-late cry for forgiveness, and I knew that a member of the brotherhood had passed, her heritage unknown even to herself.

I had killed....

Had killed Kevva.

Treyl saved me, for as I stumbled back with Kevva's blood still flowing off my coat, he dropped into a crouch and brought up still another of his strange antennae. From this one darted a line of light like fire, and where it touched, warriors withdrew. Pain and burned flesh filled the air, and their scents echoed around the still-spinning dance. Injury, injury would feed the dance and feed the rage of the warriors.

"Treyl, we must go."

"Follow me, then." His fire-antenna opened a path through the dance, and I scuttled after Treyl as he ran. He held the clevth at bay, and as we raced away I bade last farewell to the familiar tastes and odors of my clevth.

Now Treyl was all I had.

*

North and east we walked, the sun each morning red and bright to the left of the Seam of Heaven. We walked through wetlands alive with the traces of a million different creatures. I do not know how many days it took us to reach the city Cora; I was in no state to count, and those days passed one after another before me as images in dreams. Sun, trail of different beasts, wet dark soil beneath my feet—these were all I knew until we drew close enough to see and smell Cora.

Cora. Mounds, huts, maker-built edifices that towered three and four times the height of a person. The river flowed through Cora, spanned by stone and wood bridges. On the river were the square sails of great ships, the ships that sailed from Tar-Ve outward…all over the Kaan Empire and beyond, to Metla, to the Gelk lands, to the coasts of the dumb savages who traded hardwoods and odd-tasting spices for the products of our makers.

Treyl touched my chest. "Ep-Naph made the first ships, didn't he?"

"So the stories say. The brotherhood tells that the shipwrights of Tar-Ve follow instructions from the Fourth Forbidden Book every time they build." Tar-Ve, last home of Ep-Naph, is said to possess copies of all five Forbidden Books. "Only those of the brotherhood can sail the ships."

"He must have been an amazing person, Ep-Naph."

"The brotherhood reveres his memory. He was something special, Treyl. Something that will not come again."

Cora. Scents of cooking, of domesticated herds, of people living close with one another. Cries of happy children, bleating of animals. And the tang, the aroma of the brotherhood….

Without even being aware of the change, I had slipped into one of my spells. I turned to Treyl. "Why did you agree with the shamans of my clevth?"

He placed his hands on his hips. "Welcome back, Dleef."

I emanated puzzlement. "I have not been away. Why did you agree with the shamans?"

"I guess you haven't. Let me tell you, when we are in the city and have a place to rest. Antigravs or not, this backpack is heavy."

"We are not of Cora. Cora's warriors will not allow us into the city unless we are under the protection of a Coran." The city is vast, and its people of a hundred or so related clevths—none of them mine. I could find a member of the brotherhood to give sponsorship, yet that would take time.

Treyl laughed. "My backpack can take care of that." He twitched his fingers against his opposite arm, and around us grew the smell of the Cora clevths. My antennae tightened as they always do at the scent of strangers; so far, it was a friendly smell.

"Treyl, you amaze me." Then I had a thought, one that even Ep-Naph had not put into the Fifth Forbidden Book. Treyl's backpack was magical, and we could not duplicate it. Yet suppose some warriors could make themselves smell like Corans—by wearing cloaks worn by city-dwellers, or some other method that a maker might know? Why, those warriors would be able to walk right into Cora, would be able to start a war before the Corans knew what was going on.

We entered the city, and after the proper exchange of courtesies a shaman gave us the use of a room and enough food to fill us both. As usual when he ate, Treyl put his food into the backpack and sucked the mush that emerged through a tube like a youngling feeding from its parent's mouth. He swallowed some small pebbles that his pack gave him, and then I repeated my earlier question.

"You *do* cause more warriors to be formed in your clevth, Dleef. You and all the others like you. There are nearly four million worldwide."

"Others like me? You mean the brotherhood?"

"Yes. The brotherhood consists of modified warrior forms. Each of you secretes...oh, this is complicated to explain. Each of you has a particular smell which causes more adolescents to form into warrior-mods like yourselves. So the brotherhood propagates itself from among the pool of its descendants." He shook his tiny head. "We simply can't locate the center of the vector. Where the change started to begin with."

"Ep-Naph was the first of us all."

"I know. We thought that might be the answer. But the center is definitely not in Tar-Ve. It started somewhere north of here, even further than the homelands of your clevth, if Chance is right."

"I have never read the Second Forbidden Book, which tells of the life of Ep-Naph. Yet anyone of the brotherhood knows that he lived far north, in the mountains that encircle the desert of Raen. Only near the end of his life did he go to Tar-Ve. Many of his children remained in the north."

"That might be the answer. I'll have Chance run simulations."

For a time I pondered, while Treyl talked to his voices in the sky. After a long time he was done, and I was free to ask more questions. "Treyl, how am I different from my fellows? Can your backpack tell me that?"

"It's a difficult problem. You have more of a capacity to reason than do your fellows."

"Capacity to do what?"

"Reason. What you're doing now. The spells you have."

"I know that about myself. But *why* do I have the spells?"

"All of your people can reason. In times of great stress they produce a substance we call cogitin, which allows them flashes of rationality."

"I have never —"

My words hung in the air as he went on. "Of course not. Cogitin is a fragile molecule. It doesn't survive long inside the body, and even less outside. And your brains ordinarily need such a large concentration. But I've found that you warrior-mods produce a second substance, cogitigen, that causes even higher levels of cogitin production."

I had the vision of my blood seething like the breeding waters, with various smells and tastes mixing in from all directions. Bodies, the breeding waters, the seas and the winds of the world...all are alike.

"I think I understand, Treyl." We talked more, and then Treyl slept and I mulled over the things he'd said. The shamans were wrong, then, to force me to leave the clevth. The new warriors, and those younger than me...many were warrior-mods, many were brotherhood. Nothing the shamans could do would stop them from growing, from causing others to form.

And when they formed? And when there were more of us than of others? Already the sons and daughters of Ep-Naph had wrought things no makers could: the ships, the books, Tar-Ve and the Empire, the associations of clevths in Gelk and Metlan lands. What would come about when there were even more of us?

The flavor of the world was changing; every wind and every current whispered that change. When would the whisper become a roar, a shout, a drowning crescendo?

That night I left Treyl and stood on the flat baked-mud roof, beneath the stars and the Seam of Heaven, and I listened the winds. An odd breeze was blowing out of the north, bringing with it all manner of smells from upriver. Pungent jrill, sweet grass and blossoming flowers, distant strange clevths—all sent notice of their presence free on a nightwind destined for the sea.

Yet there was something else. Something like, yet unlike, the scent of the brotherhood, a smell that had called to me when I was with my clevth even before Treyl. It was a compulsion I had ignored—to go to breeding with the clevth. But tonight, alone beneath the stars with the northwind's song, I was free to answer.

The next morning I told Treyl we were going north.

"I'm not surprised. You're attuned to something, Dleef, something so subtle that we can't detect or track it. If you say we go north—then north we go."

The shaman in Cora gave us mounts: surefooted, humpbacked darets. I had to laugh at Treyl, perched unsteadily on his, as we set off along the river's west bank.

Conversation is not possible on the back of a galloping daret —the wind whips away both words and scents as soon as they are formed. We rode, and the sun moved behind us, crawling up the Seam of Heaven until our shadows pooled below us on sandy riverbank. Treyl's backpack murmured to him a little past noon, and he signaled a halt.

"Follow me." He galloped off into the high grasses and I spurred my daret to follow. In very little time we reached a mound overgrown with spring grass; next to it was a backpack just like Treyl's and a large, flat stone, fire-scored with a simple wheel design and some wavy lines. Treyl halted his daret and dismounted.

I did not need the overwhelming odor to tell me that this was the last sleeping place of one of Treyl's people.

"You didn't know Staven, did you?"

"He was killed before you arrived at my clevth. Staven was precious to you, Treyl?"

"He was my teacher. He got me this assignment. What a break! Solve the mystery of Kaa, planet of the sentient lobsters. How that would look on my record. But he didn't count on the jrill. I don't think he…he realized how much he was needed." I didn't have to smell sadness to know that Treyl missed his teacher.

I put a hand on his arm. "I'm sorry." This language is so inadequate when it expresses sorrow, compassion, sympathy. What, I wondered, do Treyl's people do? How do they avoid bursting with all the feelings that are locked within?

Treyl knelt by the backpack, touched it with an antenna from his own pack. For a long time he talked back and forth with his sky-voices, and I watched springflies twisting in their intricate dances above the grasses. Every once in a while, one could almost understand the springflies, the happywings, the other insects that filled the sky. Sometimes they were easier to understand than my friend Treyl.

"There are traces of unidentified enzymes here," he reported, "including, thirteen days ago, something that looks like cogitigen, but has a different fine structure. And strong cogitigen traces from the same period. Some of your brotherhood were here, Dleef."

An antenna-twitch warned me, and I spun to face three jrill only four daret-lengths away. "Treyl!"

There is what Treyl calls reason, caused by his funny substances swimming in the blood. And there is the state of most of my people, the waking dreamtime when one joins in the dance of the world like a skittering springfly. And both of these are good. Even Ep-Naph, who was the first of us to feel what Treyl names "thought", even Ep-Naph said that the brotherhood is not all. And the Fifth Forbidden Book nowhere mentions any improvement on the traditional methods of fighting jrill.

I remained conscious all through the fight, remained able to marvel at the way my limbs moved of their own volition, tracing paths of hate-smell in the air; at the way I pulled back from the slavering mouths, the ill-tasting claws dripping their fragrant poison. One of the darets took injury, and that saved Treyl and me—for by the time the third jrill turned away from my mount, I had killed one of its fellows and was dealing with the second. Treyl's gun ended the fight.

Breathing heavily, I stood over the dead jrill and felt hate and battle-lust wafting away on the light breeze. Treyl waved his antennae. "That other enzyme is in the air. The one that resembles cogitigen."

"It...comes from the...jrill, then?" Treyl is a strange person, able to think of his funny little smells right after a death-battle.

"From the jrill, possibly. Or from you. Maybe it's just a variant of cogitigen. Damn it, this planet is a soup, and we still haven't been able to analyze which of a million different characteristics gives it its flavor."

I scanned the horizon, looking for more jrill, almost hoping more would show up. There is a feeling of elation after a battle, and being rational made it even more intoxicating. Let whole packs of jrill come…I, Dleef, would slay them.

"Worry about it on the way, Treyl. We are riding north. Let us ride."

We forded the river at a shallow spot only a day's ride from the lands of my clevth. There was another crossing further upstream—one that my people ordinarily used. I elected to ford here because the brotherhood had a few members in the local clevth.

My people are enough related to these river-dwellers that our smells are compatible; they let me into their village and Treyl came behind me, his backpack mimicking my odor.

Mud huts, a few timber buildings, wooden pens for the herds. The village was enough like my own to make me feel a little wistful. Then, I caught a whiff of the scent I was looking for: the brotherhood.

A single person crouched in the doorway of the house that smelled like the brotherhood. Three eggs were cemented to her pled coat, each one hard and ripe and looking ready to hatch in only a greater moon or two.

"I am Dleef of the brotherhood, sister," I said to her in the speech of our kind. Her eyes fastened on me, dull and unseeing, and she drifted back to contemplation of the packed-earth floor.

"I am Dleef." I leaned forward, touched her with three arms, let her taste the exudes of my flesh. Would she not hear? Even here in the brotherhood's place, was I to be denied company? How could I be the only one who felt these spells?

Treyl waved one of his antennae between us, touched me in various places with another. "That mystery enzyme is turning up, Dleef. You're producing it." He frowned, and his sky-voices chittered at him loudly. "Her cogitigen production is going up. Ye gods, the two of you are heterodyning. Chance, are you gettin' all of this?"

The sister now looked at me again, and I knew she saw me. I sensed her quiet happiness, sensed the fact that she was aware. "I am Wreip," she said, "of the brotherhood. Welcome to house and clevth, Dleef."

More than that flowed between us, oh so much more that even Treyl's backpack could not read. Wreip learned how I had been thrown out of my clevth, how I had killed Kevva, how I had befriended this strange being who talked to voices from the sky. I learned that she was joyful with the prospect of her young hatching at last, that she had made pictures in the stars with one of the brotherhood some nights ago, that the river was running muddier than usual this time of year, that a ship from Tar-Ve had called a greater moon back and had brought some handsome fabrics. None of this was related in the language of the brotherhood, it all passed between us in the waves of wind and breath.

How must Treyl suffer, when he meets one of his people. How he must feel like bursting with all the news that he cannot relay.

Wreip led me to the river, bade me drink. I dipped my mouth into it, and the river spoke to me with myriad voices, each different and each with meaning of its own. Strong behind them all, though, was the trace that I had followed from the south. I identified it for Wreip while Treyl dipped his antennae into the river.

Wreip signaled negatives. "I do not sense it. Yet if you have followed it this far...."

"...It comes from the north, from the slopes washed by this river." Our meanings blended and we let them go downcurrent.

Treyl shook his head. "Too many strange things to identify. I think you're tracking a cluster of enzymes, and without knowing the general configuration, we'll never be able to pick it out from background noise."

"It is here." It *was*. "And I must follow it to its source." I took out my copy of the Fifth Forbidden Book, opened its pages reverently, ran my antennae over them. "It is *his*, Wreip, it comes from Ep-Naph. I am sure."

Treyl spread his arms. "Some of the clusters are bound to be similar. You're in charge here, Dleef."

Wreip smelled of puzzlement. "Come back to the hut with me." There, she opened a wood cabinet and produced a book. "This is a copy of the Second Forbidden Book. It tells of the life of Ep-Naph." She turned to the very last page of the book. "Here the scribe has recorded that Ep-Naph's body was taken by his children, loaded onto one of the marvelous ships of Tar-Ve, and taken to his homeland at the edge of the Desert of Raen. Then his clevth buried the body with due ceremony presided over by the shamans, and there it lies to this day." She pointed upriver. "This river washes the slopes of the Raen Mountains, where Ep-Naph lived. Beyond is the desert and his tomb. Go there if you wish answers about Ep-Naph."

In the air and on her skin was a trace of something she left unsaid. Others had taken this way, seeking the tomb of Ep-Naph, following a trail no one else could read. What had become of them, she did not know. None had ever returned.

One, just recently gone, was the father who bore the three companion eggs to those she carried.

"I am sorry, Wreip." I gave her my sorrow with more than voice, gave it her with all that was within me, until the air in the hut wept and I knew the furnishings would reek of it for days.

"No sorrow." The acrid odor of pain and denial filled the room. Leave me alone, it said in a voice more poignant than language, go away and let me be. How dare, how dare, how dare you to make me remember! Let me, let me be.

"She'll remain conscious and rational as long as you're here," Treyl told me. "I think this mystery enzyme triggers cogitigen production."

"Then we will leave her. And we will seek Ep-Naph's tomb. And I shall return, Wreip."

On our one remaining daret, we rode due north toward Raen.

By the time sunset came I had forgotten, and my spell was over. With dreams no more real than those of our daret before me, I clung to the galloping beast and remembered nothing

*

Rationality came back under the lesser moon and the Seam of Heaven.

"Treyl?"

"Mmm?" We were camped by the river. I lifted my antennae to the wind and realized we were further north than the lands of my clevth. We had come nearly two days' ride, then.

"Tell me about the mystery enzyme. Tell me how I was able to bring sorrow to Wreip."

"We call it procogitin. All you warrior-mods have the glands to produce it, but you're the first one we've run into who can actually make the stuff."

"I don't understand."

"Neither do we. Our biochemists are working on the problem but they don't promise a solution. Basically, this is the way Chance thinks it happened: Ep-Naph was the first warrior-mod able to make procogitin. He stimulated all those around him to produce cogitigen, which then made cogitin. And a fair number of your people became rational for long periods, in the same sort of chemical heterodyning that we've witnessed between you and Wreip, between you and Kevva."

"Treyl...."

"Sorry. When Ep-Naph died, his procogitin was removed from the scene and your society had to rely on occasional flashes of rationality that warrior-mods have in greater duration than others. That was the brotherhood."

"And?"

"And every once in a while came another Ep-Naph—one who could produce procogitin. If one like that came up in a clevth like yours, then the effects were purely local and were damped by time and distance. If one appeared in Tar-Ve, or Metla, or Gelk...Chance thinks they are responsible for the spurts of development in your culture."

"You're saying that I am another of these? I'm like Ep-Naph?"

"You're something even more special. You're attuned so well to the chemical balance of your environment that you have read traces of Ep-Naph himself, and you are being drawn to his tomb. This extra sensitivity is a mutation that Chance and other agents have traced to the extreme northwest of this continent. In you, the two mutations came together. And with every kilometer you progress toward Ep-Naph's tomb, your procogitin production increases."

"Others have come this way?"

"A few. Procogitin is a much more durable molecule than cogitin or cogitigen. It stays in the environment indefinitely. Others have been this way...and you're probably following their tracks as well."

"Where does it lead?"

"We don't know. We can't possibly read all the nuances of the chemical states. You're going to have to tell us when we get there."

"It is rumored," I said, "that Ep-Naph wrote a Sixth Forbidden Book. I have heard that this book tells that one day Ep-Naph will return and a new sun of happiness will rise over his people, and all Kaa will become one splendid people. You're saying that Ep-Naph has come back, and that I am he?"

"Don't get delusions of grandeur. We don't know what is going on. Just that more warrior-mods are being born, that your population is expanding, and that strange new changes are coming to your people."

The moon's light was cold and tasteless. "Let's ride, Treyl. I want this over."

"So do I."

*

North. The river became a stream, then a trickle, then finally a chilly spring as the land rose higher and the air grew colder. And the trace I followed was stronger.

Treyl helped me up the mountains, especially after the daret broke its leg and had to be killed. Here in the heights, where grasses and trees and flowers gave way to mosses and bare rock, Treyl was invaluable. His backpack supplied us both with water, and with food—strange-tasting yet filling.

We passed a body, and I crouched to examine it.

...Wreip's clevth-mate.

He still smelled faintly of her, smelled of the lowlands and the river. And he smelled of something else, something that made me want to rush ahead and find Ep-Naph's tomb, something that danced around the edges of my antennae and gave me a mad desire to scream until my voice shook the stars.

Treyl offered me a hand.

Dream.

Madness.

Waves of fear washed over me like the breeding waters— fear of Treyl, of the night, of the body that lay before me. I backed away from Treyl and tumbled onto the rock, hurting one of my legs.

Pain.

Fear.

Hate.

In the summer the air is sometimes so thick that it is hard to breathe, and one can choke on the leftover emotions of days passed. So I felt now, felt trapped and suffocated by fears and agonies that swirled around me.

Two ghostly images that looked like Treyl appeared next to him, and he conversed with them. I looked from one to the other, feeling awful smells and terrible growls brewing in my vitals. They had no scent, no taste; they were merely phantoms of light.

Like Treyl?

All at once the attack was over, and I moved from a packet of foul air that was swept clean by mountain breeze.

Treyl indicated the two ghosts. "Dleef, I have the honor to present Sayyid Alma deVigny and the cyborg Kwofi, both of the Kaa Cartel which protects your world."

His back pack translated their words, which were not meant for me. "Agent Treyl, we may be able to protect this world no longer. The Empire is putting pressure on us. Terran Defense is convinced that the increasing militancy of the dominant culture may prove dangerous to the Empire."

"Ridiculous."

"We know that. Terrad does not. They do not like mysteries, Treyl. Find a solution to this one before the Imperial Navy decides to set down ships and start their own investigations."

"You can't let that happen."

I crept closer, touched Treyl. "I am myself, Treyl. Let me lead you to Ep-Naph's tomb, and maybe we will find answers there."

"Did you catch that?" Treyl asked his ghosts.

"We did. Would a flier speed things?"

"We have to be on the ground, Sayyid, to read the traces and find our way. We will go as fast as we can, however."

"And we wait on two creatures scrambling over mountainsides. I do not like this. Do what you can." The ghosts disappeared, and Treyl laughed.

"Well, Dleef, I guess you're thinking that you've started to see my sky-voices yourself."

"I thought so at first. They are others like you, sending their images like...like the scents in the Forbidden Books, like the trace of myself that I send downriver whenever I cross the water."

"Astute, friend. Are you ready to continue?"

"Over the mountains and into the desert, Treyl. Follow me."

•

The Desert of Raen is a dreadful place of heat and dryness. Awful little creatures live there, six- and eight-legged beasts that scuttle in the shade of bizarre plants, waiting to strike with poisoned limbs. Treyl and I passed a few bodies, with nothing left by now but bleached pled coats picked clean of all flesh. They may have fallen to poison, to thirst, to the winds that spring up without warning…what mattered now was that they had fallen.

"No trace of any enzymes here," Treyl muttered, passing his antennae over a body.

I blinked, blinked again in sun that seared my eyes. "No, Treyl. The traces are here. We draw ever closer. Those hills in the distance, sculpted by the wind—we must go there."

Treyl shrugged. Water yield from his backpack was less than before…he told me that the air was drier, so the pack could not produce as much moisture. But the hills were only a day's walk away; we could make it easily, I thought.

Midday, and the sun sat high next to the Seam of Heaven. The Seam itself was like the glint of sun off sea, and it teased us with bright flashes in the corner of the eye.

"Dleef, I have to rest." Treyl threw off his pack and settled to the sand. I cast another look at the hills, felt wistful, and crouched beside him.

Sun….

I tumbled into dreams, clawing and grasping to stay where I was but losing my battle. Not enough procogitin, Treyl would perhaps say. I could not maintain what he called rationality. I think that the desert was too much, and after a few moments I regarded the dreams a blessing.

I was beside the river again, walking through grasslands and watching springflies dance. Then, I was next to the grave of Treyl's friend. I plunged my limbs deep into the rich, wet earth, tasted all the life that pulsed within. Life from death, as it has been and ever will be....

The mound shifted, and an arm reached up. Not a flimsy five-fingered arm like Treyl's, but a fine, slender arm coated in the star-shaped shells of pled—an arm that belonged to one of my folk.

I stepped back, and the earth opened. Forth stepped Kevva, bleeding from horrible wounds that I knew I had inflicted, half her thorax-plate hanging loose and the inner organs bulging out. She reached for me with dirt-caked hands and antennae that twitched aimlessly. She smelled like Kevva, but she smelled also like something else, like death, like decay, like... like the path I was following to Ep-Naph's grave.

I stumbled back, cried out, and found myself back in the desert next to Treyl.

Treyl....

Under a compulsion not my own, as if I were nothing but a simple warrior under the command of an excited shaman, I lunged at Treyl, tasting hate in my mouth and on my hands.

Treyl raised his weapon, and a line of fire-light touched the smallest of my limbs, burned off a section of my pled coat and barely nipped the end of the leg. I howled, and my pain filled the still desert, dripped to sink into the sand, summoned the high-flying birds who wait for death before they feed.

And dreams passed.

"I'm sorry I had to shoot, Dleef. I knew stress would trigger your cogitin production."

"I hear you, Treyl." Hate, pain, anger—still I smelled all these things. "Treyl, I wonder if you are doing me a service, or causing me harm. Let it pass. We have come here to find Ep-Naph's tomb. Let us rest, and then we will do that thing."

The sun was in the final two limbs of heaven before we left, and it was touching the horizon when we reached the hills. A few more plants grew here, and the trace I tracked was so strong that I ached with it. "This way, Treyl."

A cairn of rock, three times the height of a person, marked where Ep-Naph was buried. Some scent with meaning still clung to them: "Here lies the body of Ep-Naph. Cursed be any who disturb it."

But there were other messages, stronger messages, things I could smell that Treyl could not detect. This had brought me from the coast, and this would lead me to the next step. I ran my antennae over the rocks, and finally scrambled up the pile to one that reeked of the trace.

"Here, Treyl. This is where the message was left." I moved the rock, and all at once there were smells and tastes swimming around me. Under the rock was a tiny book, wrapped in skin and carefully anchored. I touched my antennae to its brittle pages.

As if Ep-Naph were standing beside me, I felt his presence, sensed his message in the way that all my people talked, in the way that the Forbidden Books are recorded.

"To the one who has come, greetings. You will fulfill my life. You will bring happiness to our people. You will be the messenger of Ep-Naph."

"Are you getting this, Treyl?"

"Yes." He crouched next to me, his headgear thrown back, touching the book with his pack's antenna.

I read on. "I leave behind what I have wrought at Tar-Ve. I leave behind the brotherhood, may it last. I leave behind a hope. But you, you who stand here right now, you must finish my work. There are too few of us now. Many suns after I am dead, when my descendants range all over Kaa, then my legacy can be left."

Now a different presence hovered near me, like Treyl's ghosts, like a true memory, bringing words from the past. "I am Rath of the brotherhood: scribe, and daughter to Ep-Naph. Let the one who has come pull loose the stone above this book's resting place."

I touched the indicated stone, put two hands around it, pulled. It did not move. My puzzlement flowed down the cairn; then Treyl laid his hands next to mine. "Now," he said, and again I put forth effort.

The stone pulled free—and all around it, like a bird carcass cooking long in hot water, the cairn dissolved. Rocks fell one way and another, dust rose in the stifling night. When all the movement was over, I stood with Treyl on a flat-topped rise. Twenty steps before us, desiccated and withered, brown from centuries of dirt, lay a body.

Ep-Naph.

I was drawn forward without thought, without dream, without volition or deliberation. I breathed deep, waved my antennae hungrily, ran my hands over the rocks, over the shroud of crumbly leaves, over the body.

No dream this time, images frozen since his death flowed through me. I am Ep-Naph, master of Tar-Ve, warrior of warriors, uniter of the clevths, creator of speech, he who tamed the waters. What Ep-Naph had lived, I lived now; what he had breathed, I again tasted; whom he had known, I remembered. First wondering sight of the sun against the Seam of Heaven. The breeding waters of Lake Dren, where he had taken the first painful seeds of his pled coat, and later had emerged from the shell of those tiny animals as warrior—no longer adolescent. A kill, and kills, as warriors of other clevths fell before his hands, his weapons; his plans carried out by others of his clevth. The first ships, fashioned out of tree trunks by disbelieving makers. His children. Long days of work and war that resulted in Tar-Ve, wonder of ages to come.

I had known Ep-Naph before through his words in the Fifth Forbidden Book; now I knew him through his thoughts, through his life's remembered events, through his passionate love for his people and his desire for their advancement.

The stormflood of memories abated, and I was able to do nothing but quiver weakly and gasp for breath. Then a strange calm came over me; I felt strength welling inside me like clear cold water bubbling from a spring. I faced Treyl, who was sampling the area for his backpack.

"An incredible concentration of procogitin," he said, nearly to himself. "And your system is heterodyning with his, manufacturing more...."

"I am the one he awaited." In my mind there was a curious echo. Ep-Naph had spoken in the same way to his sons and daughters, high in a tower in Tar-Ve, the night he died. "His people—my people—are more now, and his descendants are spread among them. We wait, like the pled wait in the breeding waters, until an adolescent comes by. My people and their world are that adolescent. And his body is the astringent taste in the water that triggers form change. When my world emerges from its cocoon, all will be different."

The legacy of Ep-Naph. Through his eyes I saw starved younglings—and tasted through his antennae their delight when Tar-Ve's ships arrived laden with food. This was the legacy of Ep-Naph. And I—with Treyl's help—would bring it to the world.

Treyl sunk a probe into Ep-Naph's body. "Enough procogitin here to bring rationality to all the brotherhood in Tar-Ve, in Metla and Gelk, and still have some left over. And you're producing it like mad."

I lifted my head, feeling the dry wind that would bring change to the world. Years, lifetimes would pass before this wind touched all the lands of my people—but the wind was born, and its birthcry heralded a new birth for my people.

"I will never be like the others, now. I will never have the dreamtime. Rationality is with me to stay, Treyl. And so it will be for others who see Ep-Naph."

Stars in heaven shone through the Gap. "Come, Treyl. We will take Ep-Naph with us to Tar-Ve."

*

A year later, the sun passes the Seam of Heaven in a shower of sparks while I watch from a tower in Tar-Ve. Below, in harbor, awaits the ship that will take me to the ancestral cove for breeding time. Some warriors from my clevth will ride with me this trip, even though Eylath and Treh-Nil begrudge time away from their math classes. The clevth should be together at breeding time.

Treyl cannot be here...but through the magic box he sends his ghost from far-off Terra, his homeworld. Almost I can smell the alien odor of my friend. Almost.

"I'm glad I caught you in, Dleef." Treyl has been gone for half a year, dealing with his people on behalf of mine. Danger has passed now: Treyl's people believe they understand mine, and they do not seem to fear what they understand. "I just want to wish you luck and happiness at breeding."

"I am sorry you will not be there." I miss Treyl, but in his absence he has arranged good things for my people: already technical books are being translated, and some of the brotherhood are experimenting in the southern ranges with metals. "My young will hatch in half a year; will you be back by then?"

"I'll be sure of it." There is nothing more to say in the curious limited language of speech. Although air currents in this tiny room carry all the unsaid messages I have for him, Treyl's ghost cannot read them. We exchange ritual farewells, and then the ghost vanishes.

Soon, with the tide, the ship will sail. After breeding time it will carry me back to Tar-Ve; and over years to come I will range far over the world, I and my clevth-mates, my fellows in the brotherhood, my friends from many clevths. We will further work the changes that alter the taste of the world.

Ep-Naph remains the mover of that change, in his dead body still smelling of procogitin in the center of the city...and in his living presence within me and within all who touched him, felt his memories, tasted his passions. Ep-Naph is the mover, and all of us—Treyl and his people as well—are Ep-Naph's living agents.

Soon the tide will turn. Look on the world and wonder, question, seek understanding. This is the legacy of Ep-Naph; this is the future of our people. Be happy.

•

So ends the Book of Dleef, which is also the Seventh Book, no longer Forbidden, of Ep-Naph.

Part Two:

Marching Home Again

(sixty years later)

Marching Home Again

When Johnny comes marching home again,
Hurrah, hurrah!
We'll give him a hearty welcome then,
Hurrah, hurrah!
Oh the men will cheer and the boys will shout,
The ladies, they will all turn out,
And we'll all feel gay when Johnny comes marching home.

*

I am Darruf of the Clevth of the Westering Hills; Darruf Windtaster, Darruf Riverreader, Darruf Treespeaker. Darruf Touched-By-Fate, Darruf the hands and eyes and antennae of distant King.

Since Sun first rose and touched the Seam of Heaven, my folk, my clevth, have wandered the verdant lands between cold, bitter mountains and rimmith-scented valley of the river Carioth. In all those generations, tens of tens of lifetimes, I am the first of my clevth to be Touched-By-Fate, the first to serve King. My clevth stays within the boundaries of its range, coming to sea only when the time of breeding arrives; I travel far across the wide continent, over the mountains and deep into the Chorus of the Wood, as far north as the Human settlement Es-tre-moz and beyond.

I travel, and I listen to the land. I taste the winds and the rain, the soil and the trees, the sand and the sea. I stand atop the cold mountains and breathe deeply, filling my thorax with air that tastes of distant lands across the ocean. I wade in blood-warm sea, feeling the tug of currents that have swept past other far-off shores.

In all these things, messages from the west far beyond sunset, I hear the song of other clevths and other folk, I taste the music of other lands...and I hear the voice of King. When King commands, I relay Her orders across the land. When King questions, I find answers—or find those who can find the answers. Then I give those answers to the Clevth of the Singers, who cast them into the Worldsong, to be borne upon wave and wind to the east. After a time they wash upon the Gelk shores, where Gelklings Touched-By-Fate carry them across their continent and back to King.

I learn many other things from wind and waves, many secrets of ocean and desert—of fire in the Tarveles forests, of drought in Metla, of mountains that shuffle their feet in the distant south of our own continent. I learn of abundant harvests in Shareen, of celebrations in the far north, and of the birth of a pair of twins joined at the seventh and ninth limbs in Tar-Ve.

Wind and wave also bring news that is as disturbing as it is unexpected. King—who is already older than Her father was when He died—King is coming East. She left Her home in Tar-Ve before the snows, sailed to Metla and wintered in that city. Now She sails, Her fleet of ten swift caravels casting off from Metla with the spring tide. She follows the wind, and so will be on our shores in only a few days.

Now, perhaps this is good news...and perhaps not. Here in the East, we are certainly loyal subjects of King—but we are accustomed to having a large ocean between us. She has never visited the East, never sung with the Chorus of the Wood, never supped with the strange Humans, never met in the flesh with the clevths of the East.

Now, it is true that Her father, King Dleef, did all these things and more. And it is true that He left His thoughts and His wisdom in His Fifty-Three Books—which, along with the Six Books of Ep-Naph, are the constant companions of the current King. However, it is also whispered in forest and river, in wind and sea, that our current King is not the equal of Her father.

Here in the East, we value our differences, our separation from King and from the clevths of the West, our unique song of life. And so we wait, hoping that King's arrival will not threaten these things.

From across the mountains, yet near as the beat of my hearts, the Chorus of the Wood sings that all things must change, that impermanence is the essence of life. Certainly the Humans in Es-tre-moz would agree—they welcome change, work toward it, rejoice at it. And sometimes, I wish that my people were more like them. Perhaps this new wind blowing in from the West will bring a wisdom that we sorely need.

And so we wait…in fear, in hope, in glorious dread.

King is coming. And nothing will remain the same.

*

The Fighting 307th—and with it, the Terran Empire—was coming back home to Kaa.

Shards of bright sunlight chased one another across the floor and up the distant portside wall, triangles and pentagons of brilliant white from the buttressed clerestory windows high above the vast, empty docking bay of Kaa Station.

Captain Le Galvao frowned, as much at the station's spin as at the vast expanse of fragile quartz glass. Poor design, very poor. Oh, impressive-looking as hell, a perfect stage for the Empire's return—but a single high-power laser beam would pass right through that glass and turn this esplande into an instant inferno. And without loss of pressure, so there'd be plenty of oxygen to feed combustion. Then the mad spin would finish the job, spreading fire throughout the station. Twenty minutes, he estimated, and Kaa Station would be dead.

"It's *cold*." Vida Noronha, his Color Sergeant, surveyed the empty expanse and wrinkled her nose. She shivered, retreating across the barely-perceptible shimmer that marked the boundary between station and ship. "And it smells worse than your feet, sir."

Le raised his right foot, boot polished so that it sparkled in the sunlight. "Soldier, if you don't get your ass out here and to work, it's going to *feel* this foot. I want those cameras set up *now*."

"Yes, *sir!*" Noronha snapped a salute and scrambled down the gangway. Her equipment waddled after her.

From behind him, Le heard a sardonic female voice: "What good are cameras, if nobody shows up for this shindig?" Captain Pavla Kors, two meters of lithe muscle and the best ship's commander in the Navy, leaned against the bulkhead with a spacer's habitual expression of disdain for everything.

"They'll be here," Le answered. "They asked us to come; they can't stay away without insulting Her Majesty."

"I hope you're right."

"I lived on Kaa for twenty-five years; I know how the Cartel works. Make no mistake, they're a queer bunch...but they're not stupid." Today's ceremony was geared toward the people planetside, both citizens and rebels, to let them know the Empire was back. However, the signal would also be cast out into Imperial Centcom's trackless net, to be available across the Galaxy instantly. Nobody knew if Her Majesty would be watching—if She even cared about Kaa or about anything beyond Her tulips and Her lovers, any longer—but nobody could be sure She *wasn't* watching, either. The Kaa Cartel wouldn't take that chance.

"You know best." In nearly two years of serving aboard Pavla's *Sidango*, Le had come to know the Captain pretty well; he thought she understood him also. Pavla had trusted him before, and it had always worked out. "My crew is ready to march with yours; I'm keeping Caplier and Jhonez on duty."

That left eight of *Sidango's* crew. With the Fighting 307th's twenty-one, a sufficiently-respectable crowd. "Thanks." He glanced at Noronha, who gave him a thumbs-up. Le touched a fingertip just below his right ear, activating his commlink. "Ten-*hut!* All personnel assemble in Airlock One in parade formation. Move it, you lumps, we march in ten minutes."

In less than three minutes the troops were assembled, three abreast, the 307th in dark blue Marine dress uniforms, *Sidango's* crew in Navy jet black, all with the pastel Six Globes on cap and shoulder and ankle. Le conducted a quick inspection; not a strap or buckle or strand of hair was out of place. They were good soldiers, all of them.

Le took his own place at the head of the column, next to Captain Kors and just a step behind Noronha. Almost time. "Looks as if our audience has arrived," Pavla said, nodding imperceptibly toward the docking bay. There, standing in front of a cargo crane like six dusty statues in a long-abandoned mansion, were the masters of the Kaa Cartel.

Le allowed himself a sigh. Nearly twenty years, and nothing had changed. They looked the same, perhaps a bit more grey, more faded in the sun, but eternally the Cartel. The cyborg Kwofi's crustacean limbs and scrollworked skin still gleamed in glass and gold. Balding, stooped Nobel laureate Leristec Treyl still balanced on his famous cane of pink coral. Sayyid Threesix Cinq-Mars, silver-eyed, black-maned, and only a meter tall, crouched like a Sphinx before the others. Green-cloaked Kandry Renj loomed like a minor planetoid, partially-eclipsed by the holographic shade of the reclusive Sister Julia the Blessed.

And Sayyid Alma deVigny, Mistress of Kaa, stood straight and tall in torn taffeta and tattered lace. Sayyid Alma was two centuries old if she was a day, and every second of that two hundred years was written in her face and on her hands.

The seventh member of the Kaa Cartel, discorporate but omnipresent, had been with them since *Sidango* arrived, surrounding them every moment—watching even now with all-seeing eyes: the brain of Kaa Station, the Svarth-series AI called Chance.

"Good," Le whispered. The Kaa Cartel had called for help, had specifically asked for Kaa's own unit, the Fighting 307th. After twenty years of nominal independence that was really Patalanian domination, twenty years of playing Empire against

Union while trying to avoid allying with either—now Sayyid Alma needed soldiers, and no doubt thought she could get them without Imperial entanglements. Plenty of units, Le knew, had gone mercenary. The entire sector was a patchwork of conflicting claims and pointless squabbling over imagined sovereignty. Why should the 307th be different?

But they were. His troops were loyal, loyal to him and loyal to the Empire. If Sayyid Alma and the others thought they could get the soldiers without the Throne, they were very, very wrong. And it was time they learned just *how* wrong they were.

A descending scale of tones sounded in Le's ear, and he stiffened. Half an instant after the last tone, Kaa Station's cargo hold filled with the first trumpet flourish of the Imperial Anthem, and twenty-nine feet moved forward, twenty-nine booted heels hit the deck. Before the column, Color Sergeant Noronha raised her baton high: the Imperial Colors streamed from its tip, forming a perfect holo of the Imperial Arms and then fading off into trails of light as the march moved forward.

The Imperial Anthem. As he marched, Le felt shivers play along his spine in time with the music. He'd always loved the piece: the soaring trumpets, the rumbling subsonics, the ascending strings reaching for the stars....

Nowadays it was considered unfashionable to be patriotic, childish to admit to being stirred by the supposedly-empty symbols of flag and seal and anthem. Le simply couldn't help himself; during that next-to-last movement, when all within hearing were to stand at attention, hand-on-heart—that awful stretch of near-silence, broken only by slow, soft harpstrings like the echoed voices of the honored dead—he often found his eyes misty and a lone tear trailing down his dusty cheek.

The Empire. In these days of war, plague, and universal crisis, too many had forgotten what the Empire meant. It was more than fleets and stations, more than ColReg and BuCorps, more than the sad, senile woman who occupied the Whirlpool Throne. The Empire was justice; it was culture; it was the glory of the Pax Terranica which had brought a century of peace to Mankind's teeming trillions.

Many claimed that the Empire was done, that two centuries of war and the Hlekkarian Plague had exhausted both Empire and Union beyond hope of recovery. That History, like a ticking timepiece from the Ancient Days, had at last unwound. The Galaxy, they said, was splintering; the center would not hold, and only inertia kept the pieces together. In the next decade or two, those pieces would go their separate ways, and the Terran Empire would be but a pleasant memory.

Le gritted his teeth. Not today. Not as long as loyal soldiers still served the Throne.

His column came to a halt before the Kaa Cartel; the Anthem entered its last, soaring movement and then ended in the unforgettable flourish that was as much a universal symbol of the Empire as the Six Globes.

Slowly, gracefully, Noronha turned the baton, reeling in the trailing colors, and handed it smartly to Le with a click of the heels. He, in turn, held it out to the Cartel.

Sayyid Cinq-Mars took the baton, blinking at it, and then slipped it into a pocket. "Welcome to Kaa, Captain."

Le bowed. "On behalf of myself, my troops, and the Empire, I thank you." Major Silva, digging through the Protocol database, had found a diplomatic script for taking command in a formerly-independent protectorate; Le just followed what the ship computer whispered in his ear. All the *important* work—treaties, terms of occupation, grants—had already been worked out between Chance and BuCorps. This ceremony was just for show.

"We are grateful to Her Imperial Majesty—"

A creaking, grinding sound interrupted Cinq-Mars, as Kwofi the cyborg unfolded one of its triple-jointed limbs. It waved, in a gesture whose significance was known only to itself, and its toneless, synthetic voice said, "Jeritza is on Kaa."

Le started, all thoughts of protocol instantly flown away. He echoed dumbly, "On Kaa?"

"Yes. He and his troops arrived a tenday ago. It took you long enough to respond."

Jeritza. On Kaa. For a tenday already. Major Segm Jeritza, the Patalanian Union's most notorious commander. Jeritza the Butcher, Jeritza the Demon, Jeritza who had never lost a battle, Jeritza who had killed more civilians than some planets had total population.

Five of Le's buddies rotted in jungle graves because of Jeritza. Two more had been captured, then ransomed...but what made it back didn't survive long even on lifesupport, and wasn't fit to be buried, so the pieces had gone into the reactor.

This was no longer a matter of duty, or honor, or glory of Empire. For Le Galvao, it was suddenly very, very personal.

*

Le remembered the jungle of Theras Five. Gloom, mud, stinging vines that moved like snakes and followed even the slightest trace of Human blood. Flies, slow-moving enough to pass right through defense screens and utterly unafraid of sonic fields. Pulpy things like leeches, that lived in the mud and passed through vacuum-tough pressure pants like a laser through butter. Things that gnawed and burrowed and laid eggs in exposed flesh.

And worse waited ahead....

Major Segm Jeritza, already known as the Demon, was trapped—trapped in a death-march across a hundred kilometers of hellish swamp, making for an escape boat that the Empire had already found and destroyed. Jeritza didn't know it yet, but he was an animal cornered by his pursuers.

Trapped. Desperate. More dangerous than ever.

Le hoped he would be in on the kill.

He'd seen what Jeritza did to the settlers: headless bodies bloating in afternoon sun, impaled torsos, legless and armless survivors covered with flies and begging for release. The burned, the maimed, the broken and the bleeding. The ones who had been put on lifesupport so they could scream longer. Le had seen it all, had forced himself to look when others turned away. *This is ultimate evil,* he thought. *Mark it well, Le. Remember it. Pray Father Kaal you never see it again.*

Le usually didn't relish killing—but if ever a Human had deserved to die, it was Jeritza.

Forward, drenched in sweat and waist-deep in mud, and each breath a struggle to pull enough air through overworked purifiers. Forward, weapons ready, while time and the world wound tighter, while the horizon contracted to the back of the man before him and the future shrunk to the duration of the next heavy step onward.

Until the swamp exploded.

Stupid, stupid! Jeritza wasn't somewhere up ahead, he'd been waiting for them. Preparing. Trip-lasers, triggering concealed charges. Durasteel nets dropped from overhanging branches. Screams in his ears, blood on his hands, the mud itself turning brown-red in an expanding frothy wave....

"Fall back!" Le ordered. "Pattern delta!"

Delta was comfortingly familiar, a textbook retreat. Trailing-edge troopers laid down protective fire while those in front scrambled behind the line. The injured were stimmed or sedated, defense screens were linked to dome the whole regiment. Air and space support. Make for high ground, evac with emergency antigravs, seek cloud cover, wait for midair pickup. The greenest neo could recite the formula.

Except that pattern delta was going horribly, inconceivably wrong. Half a dozen troops unaccounted for, protective fire terribly askew, no high ground in sight. The mud was bubbling —*gods, they're boiling us alive!*—and half the regiment was caught in nets. Someone, somewhere, was screaming for help and Le had none to give.

"Scrub pattern delta. Cut those nets, then evac pattern iota." *That's it, give them something to focus on. A simple job that they can do.* Then get them out of here the fastest and simplest way. Le swung his rifle, saw bright net filaments part and pulled Istas Delgado free. "Who's loose? Count off!"

The count reached twenty-one...seven unaccounted for. Dead? Unconscious? He had no way of knowing. "Evac iota!"

Le reached to his belt, opened safeties, and threw as hard as he could in the direction of the hostile fire. Then he grabbed his evac-ring and pulled.

K2 personal defense screens triggered, cocooning each trooper in a mirror-surface sphere impervious to hostile fire. Antigravs kicked in, and twenty-one mirror balls shot upward. At the same time, Le's tossed grenade went off, creating a grav warp: half a millisecond of ten thousand gees, concentrated on a single point. Swamp, trees, atmosphere, all rushed inward toward a sudden core of degenerate matter—then flew apart as that core exploded.

Le, unaware of the chaos except as a gentle buffeting, rose to the safety of the pickup ship.

Two of Le's comrades were left alive in Jeritza's hands. Those two lives, and others from the villages he'd sacked, bought Jeritza his escape. Le had watched helplessly, his forces outnumbered, as the remnants of the civilian government surrendered, turned their planet over to the Patalanian Union and their souls to Jeritza. There were other battles, an entire subsector falling to Patala, and the Empire had withdrawn in shame.

This time, Le swore, it was going to end differently.

*

My people speak to one another in the winds and water, in touch and smell, and only occasionally in sounds and gestures. Our Human friends are just the opposite; stop their ears and eyes and they are cut off from clevth and kind.

Thus, when Humans wish to converse at a distance, they send sparkling images of light, and harsh words of sound, disrupting all about them, rather than casting voice adrift in the swirl and sway of the ever-changing Worldsong. Their way seems strange to us, but no doubt our ways smell just as odd to them.

Windtaster and Riverreader that I am, I have learned to read the scents and tastes of Humans, to understand a little of their gestures and their harsh, clipped speech. I have also learned to talk with them, at least a bit. It is easier, for both sides, when we sing together rather than talking. And together, with the help of the Green Ones, understanding has slowly unfolded through our song.

This day, this glorious morning alive with the scent of rimmith blossoms and the taste of first-day-of-summer dew, ten times ten Humans are met beneath the boughs of the Chorus of the Wood, met to sing welcome to this dawn. They are led by a Human whom I have come to call by their word "friend," Kichi Wemes of Es-tre-moz.

This is one Human custom, to greet with song the first dawn of summer, which my people understand without puzzlement. Our own Worldsong, too, comes to a crescendo that welcomes Sun, welcomes warmth, welcomes the growing. Many of my folk, of clevths who live near Es-tre-moz and near the Chorus of the Wood, are gathered here to participate.

When all are singing together—my people, Humans, and the soaring Elders of the Wood, who have stood through unnumbered summers—when all voices are joined, it is a most beautiful sound. Trees and birds, clouds and wind, even Sun itself, all stop to listen and wonder.

Kichi leads us in the songs her people call "gospel," so exuberantly different from the sedate ballads of my own folk, or the cool, eternal melodies of the Chorus of the Wood. Oh, we do not know all the Human words, although we can guess at a few. "Saints" and "angels" are a mystery to us, as is "Beulah Land." But "Lord Kaal" and "Savior" seem to be Human versions of King Herself, and "Heaven" can only be the happiness that comes when one is completely immersed in the Worldsong, so that day and night pass without awareness.

With other words from Kichi's songs, we are on firmer footing. My folk know "gardens" and "friendship," we know "sun" and "rain," we know "light" and "darkness." Most of all, we know and share with Humans and Chorus the emotion that the songs call "amazing grace," "salvation," or "joy, joy, joy, joy, down in my hearts." It is a simple Human word, a sound easy to make: "Joy." But what it *means*, ah! That is profound and wondrous. It is the abiding goodness of life, the wonderment at each sunrise and sunset, the sure knowledge that life unfolds and progresses as it should.

Of all the things we share with our Human friends, joy is the greatest.

The song ends, its echoes quickly swallowed by the endless, mist-shrouded branches of the soaring Green Ones. Kichi stands before her people, her single pair of arms raised, her long mane like a dark waterfall down her back, the scent of purest Joy radiating from her—then she stops, lowers her arms, and speaks briefly with another. Kichi then steps down into the crowd, and one of the Humans' sparkling images takes shape where she stood.

I look into a place many times the size of the clearing in which we stand, a place that I recognize for I seen it often in image and have even been there twice. This place the Humans call Kaa Station, and in it live the Shades who watch over our world.

The Shades are there, standing like statues at one side of the image; but the scene is dominated by a crowd of Humans, all dressed alike. No scent, no taste, no feeling comes from this sparkling image...only the image itself, and sound.

I recognize Human music. No, it is not song, like the gospel songs that had filled this glen; it is dry and tasteless and perhaps others of my folk would not even recognize it as music. How, after all, could mere *sound* be music? No feeling, no scent, just noise. But my folk forget that Humans know the world through their eyes and ears, not through their skins. To them, music *is* just sound.

Poor, poor Humans, cut off from the real world, only occasionally to know even a hint of what music truly is.

Mere noise as it is, this Human music is at least *good* noise. It is strong, ambitious, stirring. And as the music plays, as the images of far-off Humans march across the glen, some in the audience are stirred as well. I taste echoes of devotion, of pride, of friendship. I sense that this music means more to them than simple sound, more than pleasant melody. Some among the Human crowd stand straighter, some hearts beat more quickly, some catch their breath.

Then the song is over, the marching Humans come to a halt and exchange Human words with the Shades. The Kwofi, who is the Shade physically most like my folk, speaks brief words that I understand: someone named Jeritza is here, on our world.

One cannot smell the images, so I cannot tell for sure—but by his speakings, the Human who speaks with Kwofi seems upset.

My friend Kichi, too, is upset. It is not until later, when the day is well-advanced and another round of songs has soothed her and her folk, that I realize just *how* upset Kichi is.

Although the Grove of the Wood is a two-day march south of Es-tre-moz, Human airbuses make the trip in less time than it takes Sun to progress one limb across the sky. Kichi is silent yet eloquent as she sits next to me, smelling of anger and frustration and fear. Her mood is contagious, even for Humans, and by the time we land in Es-tre-moz the entire bus reeks of a score of angry Humans.

Kichi strides directly to her studio, ignoring the greetings of those she works with. I am curious about her mood, about the visions we witnessed in the grove, about this Jeritza whose very presence on Kaa seems so important—I accompany Kichi into her building, up the dropshaft to the third floor, and into her studio.

I like Kichi's studio better than any other place in Es-tre-moz. It is a cold place, a tasteless place, a very Human place with all its winking lights and humming machines and the smell of ozone in the air—but Kichi has taken this Human place and made it more. Potted plants, open bottles holding samples of soil, the accumulated dust of years; these things soften the rough Human angles, sweeten the sharp Human smells. Often, Kichi sings as she works, and her voice is another thing that makes her studio seem less Human.

Today, Kichi does not sing. Instead, she stands at her desk and summons a Shade.

He appears before her, a short Human with hair the color of snow. I cannot be sure, but I think I know this man: I have met him in the glade, have tasted his scent beneath the spreading limbs of the Eternity Tree. He is a wise man, a kind man, a man who knows more about my people than perhaps we know ourselves.

Kichi snarls, her anger a stinging scent. "Treyl, what in space were you *thinking*? The last thing we need right now is Imperial soldiers slinking around."

Treyl—for now I know that is his name—answers softly. "Kichi, it can't be helped."

"Can't be helped! Do you have any *idea* of the effect this is going to have on the Project?"

"As a matter of fact, I—"

"Treyl, I went to school with Le Galvao. You don't know him the way I do. He's an authoritarian, a bully...mark my words, he's going to come in here with guns firing, demanding to know everything about everybody. He'll ground all our buses and slap security on our nets...all in the name of capturing Jeritza."

Treyl crosses his arms. "I think you're exaggerating."

"Go ahead, think whatever you want. You'll find out." Kichi takes a breath. "The Empire wouldn't have showed up unless we asked them to. Whose stupid idea was it, to call for the Marines?"

"The Cartel agreed unanimously...."

With a blast of rage as strong as it is sudden, Kichi pounds her fist against the desk. "I want to know who decided to interrupt ten years worth of work just to—"

Another Shade leaps into view, obscuring Treyl: Sayyid Alma deVigny, who is to the Humans what King is to my people. She is the head of their clevth, the leader of their nation, the keeper of their consciences. She is the only Human I have met who can stand tall and unawed in the shadow of the Eternity Tree. I remember her taste, a combination of ancient forest and immovable mountain.

"That was *my* decision," Sayyid Alma says. "I assume you have a problem with it?"

Kichi is scared, but hides her fear from the Shades. Only I, close enough to touch her, can taste it. "Sayyid, I think you're making a big mistake."

"The Butcher of Theras Five sets up housekeeping two hundred kilometers from our major town, and you think I am mistaken to call for help? Do elaborate, my dear."

"We're still in the early phases of the Project…but we're far enough along that Jeritza isn't a threat to us. Le Galvao *is*."

"Doctor Treyl tells me that the Project, even in its current state, will take care of Galvao and his troops. Are you telling me that he is mistaken?"

Kichi shakes her head. "We need more time."

"Time we do not have. The Empire is dissolving, Doctor Wemes. The next century will see war, plague, and famine on a scale that you and I cannot imagine. If the Project is to succeed in lessening the toll of that misery, we must move soon." Sayyid Alma raises a hand. "Captain Galvao's troops are a test. If we fail, then we know that the Project will not be ready in time."

Below Kichi's anger, there grows the pungent scent of fear. "Sayyid…I only wish you had given us more warning."

"The Cartel had no warning itself. Jeritza's arrival gave us the excuse we had been waiting for—such an opportunity may not occur again. We must needs act, and act we did. Now it is up to all of us to move ahead, to see the Project to success. I know we can count on you."

With no further ceremony, the Shades are gone. Kichi turns to her datascreens, then looks at me. "Darruf, I don't know how much of that you understood...but it looks as if we're committed. I'm going to need your help."

I nod my head, mimicking the Human gesture of agreement. "I will do what I can, Kichi."

"I hope it'll be enough."

*

Le checked the straps of his drop-pack; tight. His uniform crinkled with the tightness of a pressure-screen, wrapping his body in seven hundred grams per square centimeter of oxy-helium mix. Telltale displays in his goggles informed him that his antigrav was powered up, defense screen on standby, onboard navicomp tracking. He was ready.

Ten seconds later, as the ship arched through the stratosphere, Le felt the bottom drop out of his world. He slid through the ejection tube in two seconds, then light burst upon him and he saw the ship receding above him. Count to six, then a jerk on his shoulders as the antigrav arrested his velocity.

The next moments were an eternity of claustrophobic darkness, as Le dropped in a flaming cocoon with only a paper-thin defense screen between him and the superheated plasma of the tortured atmosphere. By the time the cocoon dissolved, Le was two klicks above a spreading forest of a thousand shades of green.

His goggles told him that he was sixty klicks from the town, and pinpointed the others of his regiment from their coded transponders. Private Thiel, as usual, was a hundred klicks off-course and dropping far too fast; Le touched override and barked orders, and was satisfied to see her plunge slow.

"Noronha, you're closest. Get Thiel straightened out. The rest of you, stay in formation."

Le dropped, protected from observation by his defense screen: a field that absorbed radar and ladar, without giving identifying echoes. The ship was similarly screened; only a few brief meteor-trails existed to give warning to any groundside observers. And even *those* were all but invisible against daylight blue.

Altitude one klick, fifty from the town. Telltales showed him that the regiment was in formation, a rough circle centered on Estremoz, a hundred klicks in diameter and closing rapidly.

Weapons check. With whispered orders, Le cycled through readouts on each system. Laser rifle, fully charged. Stunner, ditto. Personal screen generator, down 40 Kauffmans and running steady. Particle beamer, charged and ready. Rapid-fire projectile gun, loaded with 20 rounds. Sixty more ready to load. Main power unit, down to 1955 Kauffmans; auxiliary unit fully charged to 4096 Kf. Drop-pack reporting OK. Diamond daggers and bayonet, at ready.

Le smiled grimly. He was ready.

Half a klick up, thirty out from the town. Beneath him, the endless forest hugged rolling hills, a mottled carpet of misty greens and brown. Here and there, a lake or pond flashed in the sun. He tested his goggles, focusing down to a single deer-like animal that stood drinking at a pond; crosshairs bracketed the creature and Le felt his rifle tracking. Satisfied, he restored the display to normal.

The deer, unaware that it had been touched by death swift and silent, continued drinking.

Two-fifty meters up, twenty-five klicks from the town. Evidence of Human settlement: the forest thinned out into well-defined, cultivated groves amid flat robot-tended farmland. Satellite dishes and microwave relays. Emergency shelters. Civilization wasn't far.

At twenty klicks from Estremoz, Le dropped between branches and touched down in a cool, shadowed glade. At once, touchdown confirmations poured in from the others: by the end of the minute, all were down.

"Stage two," he barked, then looked skyward. Kaa Station was a barely-visible dot just to the south of zenith; magnification brought it to within a few hundred meters. *Get ready for a surprise*, he thought.

He turned his attention to his drop-pack, extended its tripod and leveled it, then punched in the go-ahead code. While the pack worked, he detached the main power unit and hooked it onto his belt. The drop-pack could run for three hours on the fully-charged auxiliary unit.

Horizon at seven klicks, plus or minus. Twenty-one troopers of the 307th, six klicks apart in a broad circle around the town of Estremoz. Line-of-sight links, simplicity itself for coherent radio beams.

And once linked, twenty-one K1 defense screen generators acted as one, throwing up a hemisphere that enclosed the town like an inverted cooking-bowl.

"*Sidango* to Galvao." In his ear, he recognized the voice of Lieutenant Riv Sanachi, *Sidango's* Comm officer, on a sealed-beam ultrawave circuit. Only ultrawave could penetrate the defense screen.

"Go ahead."

"Kaa Station reports total loss of signal from Estremoz and wants to know what the fuck you're doing down there."

"Acknowledged." Stage two had worked: Estremoz was now electronically isolated from the rest of the planet. "Tell Captain Kors she can bring the ship down at her discretion. We'll meet her in the central plaza."

"Kaa Station wants to talk to you soonest."

"Roger that. Tell them I will report when I have a spare moment." He snorted. "No, strike that. Tell them I am incommunicado and will report in asap. Pretty it up."

"Acknowledged. And out."

"And out." He thumbed to the regimental frequency. "All right, slackers, rest break's over. Time to get to work. Last one in is on three weeks' report." Le watched their telltales scramble, and allowed himself a grin. Good kids, each and every one of them. He'd be sure he was the last to show up—but still, the threat would make them *fly.*

He left his drop-pack and the intangible defense screen it generated, and started off at a brisk trot toward the town.

*

As I move through verdant forest and across spring-swelled streams, Worldsong is alive with news, with pleasure, with joy. A million voices bring knowledge across the spine of a continent, happy knowledge borne on wind and wing, in rain and dew: King has arrived in the East. Even now, She marches from clevth to clevth, bringing Her sacred touch to all.

Where once there were misgivings, now there is only joy. King is here! All rejoice: maker and farmer, herder and carrier, warrior and runner and shaman alike. Out of the West, out of the sunset, She has come, She who is Leader of Leaders, Mother of All.

An entire land sings, in truesong and not pale Human mockery of song: grass and trees, soil and cloud, all are alive with the scent and taste of joy.

I would that Kichi could share this song.

I find myself among the Chorus of the Wood, in the very glen where Kichi and her folk sang so recently. I walk forward, stepping for a moment away from Worldsong and into the cool, quiet melodies of the Wood. The life of the world intrudes very little into this place; there is only sun and fallen leaves and simple creatures entirely unaware that they live and die in an island of bliss among the world's clamor.

Deeper I go into the Wood, further Worldsong fades behind me. Am I still uneasy, unwilling to face King's arrival? Or is it the disturbance I sense in Kichi and the other Humans, which drives me into this shadowed coolness? It is not my place to say. I only know that I retreat, and that the Chorus of the Wood sings peace within my heart.

I walk until I stand at the roots of the Eternity Tree.

The Eternity Tree is the oldest of the Chorus, oldest of the Wood, perhaps the oldest living thing in the world. She was here before my people first came East, here before Worldsong was sung, here before the mountains were raised.

Here in the depths of the Wood, where the current of Worldsong slows to lazy, silent pools—here it is sometimes possible to sing with the Eternity Tree, to sway with her limbs, to breathe in the gentle susurrus of her moving leaves and the stately, hypnotic swim of ever-changing colors in the depths of her substance. Here it is sometimes possible, even, to talk with her.

For the Eternity Tree, like all her siblings of the Wood, does speak. Not as my people speak, nor as the Humans speak; the Eternity Tree speaks in the way that the wind speaks: to the ears; in the way that the sunset speaks: to the eyes; and in the way that music itself speaks: to the soul. Hers is the Inner Voice, the quiet echo or the scent on the verge of sensation. Turn too quickly, listen too hard, and you will miss it. Be at peace, and you will wonder how you ever overlooked it.

(*Little One, your hearts are in turmoil. The Worldsong of your people is agitated. Much fear and anger from the Humans. Sing to me of these things.*)

I sing to her of all that I have witnessed; of the confused smells of the Humans in Es-tre-moz; of King's progression across half the world with Her thousands of followers. If I am less than clear, if my song is muddled and my meaning jumbled, then the fault is mine, not that of the Eternity Tree. For I still do not understand what is going on in the world.

Yesterday, there were bright flashes like heat lightning in the direction of Es-tre-moz. Today, there is consternation in the small Human band at the BioStation on the edge of the Wood. The Humans do not seem to know what has happened in Es-tre-moz.

There is the sound of leaves shuffling in a great wind, although the air is still. I shiver, hearing the Eternity Tree's words in my head. (*Great changes are coming to Kaa, Little One. Your biochemical Worldsong swirls like a powerful storm. The Humans lie at the eye of this vortex. When the storm passes, both races will be altered. And not even the Wise can say if these changes are a good thing, or a bad.*)

I falter, lose her for a moment...then feel the endless depths of her power upholding me. "This has to do with the Humans' Project. And with Kichi. And with me. But what has it to do with King's arrival?"

(*The language of your Worldsong is not easily deciphered. One must live very fast indeed, to keep up with its fluctuations. More than any other world in the heavens, Kaa is a single organism, knit together by air and water and the chemicals of life. That organism responds to stimulus, and who can gauge that response? Humans disturb the Worldsong with their Project; King becomes discontent and leaves for the East. There is a connection, Little One...but even the Wise cannot its subtlety reckon.*)

"What am I to do? Return to Es-tre-moz?"

(*Your King summons you, Darruf Touched-By-Fate. Why do you not acknowledge Her call?*)

Now it has been said, the thing I have been trying to deny. Yes, even in the stillness of the Wood I can feel King's appeal, drawing me toward the mountains which She approaches from the other side. No, I have *not* acknowledged her call, not even to myself.

I am afraid.

(*Afraid of what, Little One?*)

The storm.

(*Go to Her.*)

But Kichi may be in danger. *She* needs me. King has a thousand servants.

The Eternity Tree says nothing, and I feel her power recede like departing tide. I gasp for air, tasting the infinite voices of my world in a quiet but rising chorus.

King is coming. And I must go to Her.

*

Kichi Wemes stormed into the Mayor's office with all the righteous force of a scorned typhoon. The dark-paneled doors barely snapped open fast enough to clear her imposing bosom, then seemed to give a sigh of relief as they slid shut behind her.

Nils DeAndrade, more farmer than Mayor, cowered behind a terminal at the edge of the room. DeAndrade's hardwood desk, taken over by a detailed holo-map of the land around Estremoz, was dominated by a short, muscle-bound man in Imperial Marine Corps battle gear. His face was carved from basalt, his hair the color of granite, his eyes cold as cometary ice. A scarred faultline ran across his left cheek from eye to chin. It had been a long time, but she still recognized Le Galvao.

Kichi took a deep breath and, with all the power of thirty years of voice training, demanded, "When are you going to drop this containment field and let us get back in contact with the rest of the planet? You're holding up important research."

The soldier grinned. "Hello, Kichi. Mayor DeAndrade told me you would show up sooner or later. I'm glad you came— you're one of the things I've missed most."

"What is that supposed to mean?"

His eyes softened just the slightest. "Don't tell me you've forgotten?"

"No." Damn. Twenty years or more since she'd seen him last. Theirs had been a teenage romance, puppy love, the kind of on-again, off-again affair that Kichi and her school friends had always called "a two-month disaster." It had lasted about that long before the requisite fight had shattered it. They'd both escaped relatively unharmed, even laughed together about it on Graduation night.

Teenage love. A distant echo of the real thing. Silly, shallow, inconsequential. He paled in comparison to any later lover. Still...he was special. He was the first.

"I guess it's good to see you again. It's a surprise. I...I thought you were...." She didn't finish.

His grin remained. "Gone forever? Dead? Not quite, although a lot of people have tried." He lowered his eyes. "It's good to see you, too. What are you doing with yourself?"

"I lead the Estremoz Gospel Chorus. And I'm a biochemist, working with Doctor Treyl and the natives on a special project." She took a breath, steadying her resolve. "That's what I came here to talk to you about. Your containment field is wreaking havoc with our schedules. You've got to drop it."

His grin faded. "Not yet."

"When?"

"A day, maybe two. I've got my people out searching the village. As soon as I'm sure that Jeritza isn't here, I can release the blockade."

Kichi shook her head. "That's unacceptable."

"I'm sorry you think so. But I know how Jeritza operates, and I'm the ranking officer here. Like it or not, I'm in charge of this operation. As long as—"

"I don't care if you're the Empress' bastard son by the god Brandix himself; you just don't understand what this planet is all about."

"Kichi, it's *you* who don't understand." He was doing a remarkable job of holding his temper, which made Kichi feel foolish in her own anger. "You haven't seen what Jeritza does. You don't know what he's capable of. If a few days of inconvenience is all that Estremoz suffers, then you ought to be thankful. We'll finish up the search here as soon as we can, and then we'll be out of your way."

Kichi steadied her breathing. He was making every effort to be sensible. Perhaps he would listen to reason. "I know more about Jeritza than you think. His war crimes have been in the news a lot around here. I know about Theras Five and Califhar and Tenipda Chel and all the rest." Suddenly aware that her hands were shaking, she laid them flat on the desk. "What you don't see is that *Jeritza isn't a threat to Kaa.*"

"I've been fighting the man for a decade; I think I know more about him than—"

"But you don't know about Kaa!"

"I was born here."

"That doesn't mean anything. You've been gone for twenty years. You don't know about the Project."

He raised an eyebrow. "Go on."

Would he listen? "You know that this planet's whole biochemistry is unique. The natives, every form of life on Kaa, all communicate constantly by sophisticated chemicals in the environment. Enzymes, complex proteins, things that behave like viruses...it's symbiosis on a scale we can't even begin to imagine."

"This isn't news to me."

She ignored his comment. "Have you ever wondered how it must feel to the natives, to be able to perceive the world the way they do? In a way, I think it must be like music: a symphony of taste and scent, a voice in every wind, a note from every living being. Between themselves, total communication. They share emotions, memories, every facet of consciousness."

Le glanced away, then back. "I can give you five more minutes."

"Then *listen.* Doctor Treyl wondered if it wouldn't be possible to give Humans that same sort of perception. To make us sensitive to what goes on in the environment. To make us *that* attuned to one another. That's what the Project is all about."

She could see him struggle with the concept. "And you think you can do it?"

"We've had some success," Kichi answered. "Tailored bacteria and protozoans in the bloodstream. Organisms that can read the biochemical code of Kaa, can translate that code into enzymes and proteins and hormones that our bodies understand. Other organisms that do the reverse, and broadcast the chemical cues." She fumbled for a metaphor. "When you talk by ultrawave, a computer turns your voice into ones and zeros, then transmits them to a receiver tuned the same. The receiver turns those ones and zeroes back into speech. Kaa's biochemical code is the ones and zeroes." She waved at the map display. "Half of the Human population of Kaa is working on the Project. Chance has dedicated three lobes of its brain to the models. We have natives working with us, and a grove of Hlutr helping us out with the biosynthesis. They may look like trees, but they're the Galaxy's best natural biochemists."

"Kichi, this is all very fascinating, but I don't see what it has to do with Jeritza."

"*Every*thing. Suppose you're Segm Jeritza, and you get it into your head to attack Estremoz and burn a few thousand civilians. And suppose you can *feel* everything that those civilians feel—every wound and every scream, all the terror and the pain, they all hurt *you* just as much as them. Do you think you're going to be able to continue?"

He thought for a moment, then shook his head. "You don't know him. And even if what you're telling me is true, it's too late. Jeritza's on-planet and has been for more than a tenday. We don't have time for your Project to finish up, much less for the effects to spread to him and his crew."

Kichi sang a quick chorus of "Sweet Hour of Prayer" in her head before answering him. "Le, you just don't get it, do you? The Project is under way even as we speak. We have a vector based on the influenza-A virus and a Kaanese free-floating microbe; the Cartel was going to have it released yesterday." She sneered. "Your defense screens might stop lasers and radio, and your detectors might keep people from crossing the line—but there's nothing you can do to keep out microorganisms."

"I don't believe it." His voice was flat.

"Fine, *don't* believe it. It's happening anyway. The Project labs are in the forest a few dozen kilometers south of Birkham. There's a river that opens into the sea thirty kilometers from here. And several colonies of avianoids that range this far north. If the vector didn't hit Estremoz by yesterday nightfall, I'd be very surprised."

"You can't even know that your labs actually released this stuff."

"Get with it, Le. I *know*." Kichi thrust her Junoesque chest forward. "If you concentrate, you can feel it: like a sense of *deja vu*, just on the borders of your mind. Don't you feel my emotions? Don't you feel Nils being puzzled over there in the corner? Don't you feel all the microbes sliding around in this room, a gritty sort of feeling in your palms and the soles of your feet?"

Just a moment, an instant, the granite cracked and his eyes widened. Then he seemed to take possession of himself. "All right, I'm sure you're telling the truth. But I can't rely on your Project when the safety of this whole planet is at risk."

"But…." What? There's more. We don't know for sure what additional factors Chance programmed into the chemical matrix, what the Elders of the Wood have dumped into the Worldsong. We can't be sure what's going on with the natives. This is just a first step along the Project road, a step that we took before we were ready.

No. He wasn't going to listen. And she had enough work to do.

"I'm sorry, Kichi," he said. "Your five minutes are up. I'll have one of my people notify you as soon as we're ready to drop the screens."

"Right." She spun and walked out. On the way back to her lab, she pulled out her compterm and dictated a message to be cast out into the Estremoz commnets. "The Gospel Chorus will meet for an evening concert at sunset tonight in Central Square. All citizens are welcome." Close up, through the agency of the music, she'd be able to feel how successful the vector was.

By sunset, everyone in town should be infected.

And by next sunrise…who knew?

*

King's camp stretches from horizon to horizon, from mountain's foot to river's edge all acrawl with people. I have never before seen so many people in one place. I did not fully understand that there *were* this many people in the world.

The air is alive with sensation. With music. With joy. King is here, King has touched each and every person in the valley. They sing the song of King, they rejoice to be in Her presence.

It has taken all of a day for me to march to this valley, all of a day following King's scent—which is also King's will—upstream and to the very foot of the mountains. My limbs are sore, I am hungry…the heady brew of joy intoxicates me and I stumble through the crowd, being pushed this way and that, moving in an ever-contracting spiral that is taking me to the great central tent where King abides.

All about me are males, females, children, of all ages and all types. As I move among them, I read their stories, in glimpses like the momentary illumination of lightning on a dark night. Some have come with King from the West; some have joined Her march as She passed by their clevths. Others, again, have been drawn from far lands, have walked for days and days and days to come here and join the great march.

When King's business here is done, some will return to their clevths. Others, Touched-By-Fate as I am, will wander across the lands in service of King and Her successor. Many will stay with Her, will follow Her back into the West, to Tar-Ve or wherever She leads, abandoning farms and villages, clevths and children, lives they have known and people they have loved.

And still others will remain untouched, unchanged by King's passage. Some of those wander dumbly now amidst the crowds, with antennae drooped and eyes glassy.

As I approach the center of the valley, the news I read from those I pass becomes dire. The rough winter, the sea voyage, the long march have all been hard on King. Not in the best health to begin with, She has grown weak. Whisper becomes rumor becomes furtive gossip...becomes truth. King is dying.

I move closer, drawn by King's summons and propelled by the people around me. And now that I am within sight of King's great tent, now that it looms only a few handspans away, the people I touch are King's close servants, Her intimates, Her ministers. Those who share the air She breathes, who touch Her every day. Although I tremble with my own temerity, they seem to know who I am, and each pushes me toward the next, as if they have been waiting for me. Perhaps they have; I am Darruf Touched-By-Fate, Darruf who is known to King and to Her ministers. Darruf, who has in his time served as ears, antennae, and voice of King. While I have never met Her in the flesh, I have tasted Her orders and her questions in the wind and the rain, as She has tasted my replies.

We are old friends, King and I.

The tent opens, and I step into the presence of King.

Surrounded by Her people, King rests on a magnificent divan in the center of the tent. The very fabric of the tent drips with Her will, Her memories, Her experience. Worldsong eddies around Her, a magnificent tide that ebbs and flows continuously, a delicate spiderweb that reaches out to all corners of the globe. And at the focus, at the center, is King Erreaf: She who knows all that occurs in the world. King holds the very soul of our folk in her limbs. She *is* the soul of our folk.

She raises Her antennae, twitches them in my direction, then turns Her eyes to me. "Darruf Touched-By-Fate," she says. "Come to me."

I walk to Her, She reaches out to me, and we embrace.

Worldsong mounts to a shattering crescendo, and it seems as if King and I, together, are carried into the sky on the back of a wind that could move mountains. Still in the tent, it is as if we sail over the world in the manner of Human airbuses, and I regard the infinite texture of the Worldsong itself spread out like a blanket before me. I perceive the world as King perceives it, as the Human Wise Ones perceive it in their orbital home, as the Eternity Tree must perceive it.

We descend, together, to the divan we never left. In the space of a few short breaths, I have seen the totality of the Worldsong; I have seen the creatures of this world arrayed each in its proper place. I have seen what the Worldsong wills for me, for my people, for the Humans and for the Chorus of the Wood.

And at last, I know what I must do.

*

Kichi removed her goggles, tossed them onto her desk, and rubbed her eyes. Her muscles were tight, her eyes burned, and she was no nearer to understanding.

The concert had gone badly. She'd been singing long enough to recognize a turkey show, and last night's concert had been the turkiest. The audience was cold, unresponsive; the performers shared a common stage but certainly not a common melody or rhythm or even key. People were snappish, irritable, and what she'd hoped would be a growing-together experience nearly turned into a riot before Mayor DeAndrade ordered everyone to go home.

And the Project...something was wrong with the Project. It wasn't working the way it should. The concert was proof of that. Oh, there was some sensitivity to the emotions of others—

but nothing at all like the wide-open communication the Project was supposed to create.

Damn it, where was Darruf? Caught outside Estremoz when the containment fields came on, no doubt, and unable—or unwilling—to return. And he had business of his own, what with his King arriving on this continent and all...but still she missed the big arthro. He was always able to give her problems a different perspective.

Her compterm beeped. "What?" she demanded.

The comp voice was dry and tasteless. "Captain Galvao has announced the imminent lowering of the containment field."

"What time is it?"

"Two-thirteen A.M."

A full half-day ahead of schedule. Le was certainly not wasting his own time.

"Acknowledged. Get me in touch with Leristec Treyl as soon as that field is down." Kaa Station, in Clarke orbit above Estremoz, kept the same hours as the town; Kichi rather meanly hoped Treyl would be asleep so she could enjoy waking him.

Treyl, however, was with her so quickly that she wondered if he'd been trying to call her. His holographic ghost unfolded in the air before her, neatly bisected at the waist by the lab table.

"Kichi, thank the gods we got through. There's trouble."

"You're telling me? Treyl, something's gone wrong with the Project. I'm not seeing anywhere near the effect I should. I've scanned for our tracers, and they aren't present in one-tenth the concentrations Chance predicted. If we don't—"

"Kichi, will you shut up and listen to me? We've been working on the Project and we might have some information for you, but that can wait. Right now, I need you to get out to Site Two as quickly as you can." Site Two, the village called Birkham, was the second largest Human settlement on Kaa—and the headquarters of many of the Project's key biologists.

"What's happened?"

"Jeritza hit there a half-hour ago. We've lost contact with the village."

"I'm on my way."

*

From the center of Birkham, Le could see the whole village just by turning his head. There wasn't much left. Buildings that had been houses, labs, a church...all were empty shells, gutted and smoking in the fire-red light of dawn. Bodies—ninety-six of them by official count, but he was ready to admit that his troops may have missed some, or mismatched pieces of others —lay stacked in an open space in front of the church, where Le imagined that they'd laughed and chatted and visited with one another after services every tenday.

Not any more.

Kichi, red-eyed and looking like she hadn't slept for a month, stood before the mound of corpses with half a dozen Kaa Humans flanking her; citizens of Estremoz who had shown up unannounced at the charnel house that Birkham had become. There were a few natives, as well, looking like a cross between mantis and lobster; they'd come from the forest surrounding Birkham and had ignored Le and his troops.

The six corporate members of the Kaa Cartel, too, were present by holo, frozen in their accustomed positions and silent as the ghosts who would forever haunt this place.

With the rising sun painting the sky blood-crimson, Le ordered his people to assemble before the church. Those who were not occupied with defense, came at double-time and fell into ranks at full attention. They'd faced cleanup duties like this all too often in the past, but this time it was different. For every one of them, no matter where they'd been in the last two decades, Kaa was home. Only Lt. de Ornelas had lost family at Birkham—a brother and two nephews—but each of them knew that it could have been parents, siblings, cousins, childhood chums....

Kichi raised her arms to the rising sun, struck a tambourine, and broke into song. Noronha, alert as always, spotted her with an amplifier and her voice boomed out over the still forest:

I was standing by my window
On a cold and cloudy day
When I saw the hearse come rolling
For to carry my momma away.

The others, Human and native alike, joined her on the chorus:

Will the circle be unbroken,
By and by Lord, by and by?
There's a better home a-waitin',
In the sky Lord, in the sky.

The song progressed, and Le found himself joining the chorus, more strongly with each repetition. He was not a religious man, he didn't believe in the gods and eternal life and all that nonsense—but he had seen how much of a comfort belief and prayer could be to those who *were* religious. And this singing, this sharing of grief, *was* comforting.

One by one the seats were emptied,
One by one, they went away
Now that family, they are parted.
Will they meet again someday?

With tears on his cheeks, Le sang along with the others, with the Fighting 307th as well as the civilians and natives.

*

One of Le's people brought Kichi a datachip with the ID's of all the Birkham dead. She slipped it absently into her purse, wondering what she was supposed to do with it. Mayor DeAndrade would know. He'd want to notify next-of-kin, and all the rest.

There was a small waterfall in the woods not far from Site Two, a tree-shadowed glen where a tiny brook dropped three meters   into a shallow pool before continuing its way down toward the river and, ultimately, the ocean. Earlier settlers had cleared a path and fitted the site with unobtrusive benches carved out of native hardwood; now Kichi was grateful for their effort. She couldn't face the remains of Birkham, the awful work of incineration and sanitation that faced Le's troops. Let them come get her, if they needed her.

"Kichi." Treyl's image formed in the dancing spray.

"Go away, Treyl."

"We need to talk. Chance and Kwofi and I have been working with Site One, and we think we can shed some light on the Project's failure."

Kichi shook her head. "Condemn it, Treyl, it was supposed to *work*. It was supposed to prevent things like this from ever happening."

"I know. I'm sick about it. We all are."

"I'm so sorry for you," Kichi snapped. "The people of Birkham are *dead*. And it's our fault. All of us." She threw a stone into the pool. "Damn it all, Jeritza wasn't supposed to be able to do this again. He was supposed to feel their pain." She clenched her fists. "The pain was supposed to *kill* him before he went this far."

"I'm sorry. You're right, it *is* our fault. Mine more than yours...more than anyone's." Water hid his face for a moment. "But Kichi, nobody else did any better. Captain Galvao was on-planet with a full division of Imperial Marines; we've got a Navy ship working with them in orbit. *They* couldn't stop Jeritza; we have no reason to expect that they'll be able to stop him next time. The Project is our only hope. And if we're going to make the Project work, we're all going to have to work together."

"I'm tired, and I'm filthy, and there are a hundred dead people half a kilometer away from here that I'm going to have to face again. I'm sick of the Project and I'm sick of *you* and I'm sick of everything." She lowered her eyes. "Maybe we don't deserve to live, after what we've done. Maybe Jeritza is the Lord's way of telling us that."

"You're not the first person to tell me that. And maybe you're right. I certainly can't blame you for thinking that way." Treyl took a deep breath. "But what if it isn't *us*, Kichi? What if Jeritza decides to attack someone else next?"

Kichi shivered. "What do you mean?"

"There are half a million natives gathered not a hundred kilometers from Birkham, including the King. They're marching toward the Wood."

Cold terror grabbed Kichi's throat. "He wouldn't."

"The man's insane. He just might."

"All right." She fumbled for her compterm. "I should get back to my lab. No, I'll go on to Site One. I need to compare notes with the people there. Meanwhile, what do you have?"

"Kwofi's been looking into your notes at Estremoz. You didn't test cogitigen and procogitin concentrations in the environment."

"Does it matter?" Cogitigen and procogitin were two of the thousands of enzymes that the natives produced; more stable than most. They had a tendency to build up in the environment. There was a whole class of native microbes, parasites on the natives, that built their life-cycle around the two enzymes.

"Chance thinks so. In theory, procogitin acts as a catalyst, enhancing a dozen of the reactions on both sides of our transmission. Cogitigen does the same with fewer reactions. They're both important."

"What kind of concentrations is Chance looking for?"

"It's guessing one to two parts per million to get the ball rolling. But two to three *hundred* ppm is what it really wants to see."

"You don't get concentrations like that except in native cities." She frowned. "Treyl...we can't synthesize procogitin. The only source is the natives themselves."

"That's right."

"Then you're telling me that we built this whole elaborate structure, that only works when we're in the middle of a native city?"

Treyl's image wavered; next to it appeared the *fortune rota* icon used by the AI Chance. Tonelessly, Chance said, "The original experiment was designed for execution on the surface of Kaa. The early phases of the Project rely on procogitin and cogitigen as catalysts because building our own catalysts into the system would have been prohibitive in time and expense. We expect, and the Hlutr concur, that a sufficient concentration of these enzymes will trigger a series of mutations in the Project micro-organisms. With guidance, we can then drive these mutations in a direction that will eliminate the Project's dependence on procogitin and cogitigen."

"So once we have a concentration of two to three hundred ppm," Treyl asked, "We'll get an evolutionary spiral?"

"Exactly," Chance answered. "The end result of that spiral will allow the Project to spread beyond Kaa by direct Human-to-Human infection."

"I don't like this," Kichi said. "King is marching toward Site One with half a million followers. Procogitin and cogitigen levels are going to go sky-high. Chance, this looks too carefully planned."

"I cannot precisely calculate the influence of the Hlutr, or our own work, upon native socio-behavior. I will note that the preliminary timeline assumed that Site One would release the Project Phase One organisms six days from now. The arrival of Major Jeritza disrupted our schedule."

The peaceful green forest and lazy waterfall seemed suddenly to be closing around Kichi, cutting off her light, her air, and any chance of escape. "I feel like we're all being maneuvered into something that we don't completely understand. Once the Project starts mutating, how are we going to be sure we can control what it becomes?"

"The Hlutr assure us that—"

"Of course they do. Haven't either of you wondered that they're the only ones who seem confident?" Kichi felt an unheard melody pushing her along, even though she didn't know the song. It was one thing to fake your way through a hymn you didn't know...quite another to do the same thing with the fate of a world.

But could she stop it? Could anyone?

Should she even try?

*

With identities established and personal effects collected, the only job that remained to the 307th cleanup crew was incineration. It was a fairly standard procedure: three portable screen generators established an inside-out defense screen around the pile of bodies, then laser gunners targeted the pile and fired. The high-energy beams passed through the one-way screens, but radiation from inside was reflected, concentrated. Three minutes of such mounting hell was enough to cremate anything once living, but the regulations called for ten minutes to be on the safe side.

Le left Warrant Officer Delgado in charge of the operation and went in search of Kichi. He found her in the woods, sitting on a bench and working furiously at her compterm. He cleared his throat and she looked up.

"I wanted to let you know how sorry I am that this happened," he said. It sounded lame.

Kichi narrowed her eyes. "I suppose I'm supposed to admit that you were right."

"No. I *wasn't* right. I came back to Kaa to stop this sort of thing from happening." He lowered his gaze. "I'm glad Mama and Papa aren't alive to see this. I should have been ready for Jeritza. I should have had forces here to protect Birkham."

"Both of us have made mistakes, then. Let's just leave it at that."

"We're going to stop him, Kichi. I promise you that. I've called for reinforcements from the Empire. One way or another, we'll get him."

She slammed her compterm down on the bench. "And still you haven't learned. An eye for an eye, right? He hurt you, so you hurt him. And so it keeps going. Nothing's enough for you. You break bodies and burn children and carry war with you like a plague of insanity from world to world and across history. Before this it was the Imperial Formation Wars. Before that, the Colonial Wars. Population Wars, Cold Wars, World Wars…the toll of the hurt and the abandoned and the dead just keeps on rising. Us against Them, century after century. Your violence never solves anything, never ends the wars." She spat. "Why can't you just go off and play soldier on some other planet? Why did you have to come back to Kaa to begin with?"

Le held his tongue, not knowing exactly how to respond. Of course she was angry, she needed to lash out at someone…and he was a convenient target. But he didn't know what he could say to make her feel any better.

After a few moments, Kichi sighed. "I guess I didn't mean that. I apologize."

"No, you have every right."

"It's just…Le, I'm so angry. At myself, at the Project, at Treyl and Chance and all the rest of them. And now you come here and talk about stopping Jeritza—all I can see is more dead bodies, an unending line stretching from here to the end of time."

"It's understandable. Uh, listen…I'm going to need to talk to you at some point, soon. Our next priority is to figure out where Jeritza is likely to strike next, so we can be ready for him. I understand that Birkham was one site for this biological project of yours—I'll need you to point out the other sites on a map and tell me a little about them."

She stared as if not believing him. "We know *exactly* where he's going to strike next. I can even make a guess at *when*—he seems to like the early morning hours. That's what

Chance predicts, based on the pattern of his previous attacks. I just hope that gives us enough time."

"What are you talking about?"

Kichi stood. "You're going to try to stop Jeritza. And I'm going to do my damnedest to stop both of you before it comes to that. So come on, we've got work to do."

*

An hour after Sun rises, King's great procession is ready for the march. All tents are folded, rolled, stowed on the broad backs of pack-darets or in the great wagons that have come all the way from the West. All children are fed, quieted, lifted in parents' arms or taken by the hand. All fires are doused, all waterskins filled. King, reclining on Her divan and borne by six strong volunteers, is lifted. Twelve abreast, King's folk stand ready.

Scouts at the head of the column give the signal, and the march commences.

I walk next to King, holding two of Her hands in mine so that we can continue our communion. My limbs move on their own, by habit; my mind is elsewhere.

Well I know this region through which we move, highlands descending in gentle slopes to the cool shadow of the Wood. Soon the great trees arch over us, and we walk on sweet-smelling loam as we feel the presence of a myriad tiny creatures: grubs, worms, insects, the fleet-footed rodents and the flapping birds.

Delight. Many of these people have never seen a forest like the Wood; they are ignorant of its pleasures. A child, joyful and exuberant, brings King a garland of flowers; though She is weak, King allows the treasure to be placed on Her head. A young farmer brings King a jug of clear, cold water from one of the many streams; King drinks, and is happy.

Soon enough, we come to the first of the Chorus of the Wood. Here, at the base of the magnificent Elder One, King calls for a halt. Her bearers lift Her from the divan and set her next to the Great One's trunk. I take King's hand, and together we sing, sing the joyous peace of Worldsong, sing in harmony with the Chorus. Tell the Eternity Tree, that King is coming. She has arrived in the East at last, and She is coming to you.

(All of you are welcome, Little Ones. Your place has been made ready. Come in joy.)

Half a million of our people will not fit within the clearing that surrounds the Eternity Tree; King speaks, and the order is given for Her followers to disperse throughout the forest. Happy one and all, they comply; here they will wait until She needs them.

King, however—wracked by coughing fits, but possessed of an inner peace that swaddles us all—King continues east, toward the Human lab, the clearing, and the Eternity Tree. We, who are Her faithful followers and also Her companions, travel with Her.

*

As soon as she stepped out of the airbus at Site One, Kichi knew that the Project was working. Bev Machado, the brilliant woman who was Site Coordinator, met Kichi with her customary hug; the imprint of Bev's arms lingered like a breath of perfume as the woman withdrew. Kichi felt closer to Bev than ever before, the sort of closeness that she usually felt only when she was on stage singing with someone.

They walked to the low wooden bunkers that housed the Site One labs; Le and his people hit the ground and fanned out, weapons ready. "Playing soldiers to the end," Kichi said drily.

"I'm not sure if this is the end, or just the beginning," Bev answered. "Just wait until the vector gets really working for you. It's a completely different world."

Inside the bunker was a scene of contained chaos. A dozen and a half workers—there had never been any more at Site One —were hunched over terminals, frantically working with sensors, adjusting equipment. A stoppered beaker flew by, tossed by a tech at one end of the room; at the other end, a hand shot up just in time to catch the bottle.

For a moment, Kichi simply stared...then she realized what was so odd about the picture. This group was operating in almost complete silence, in total concentration on the tasks at hand. No casual conversation, no whispered comments, no whistling or humming or singing—only a few rustles and an occasional electronic signal from a terminal broke the quiet.

Bev nodded. "Unnerving at first, isn't it? All the random chatter is still going on...it's just in here." She touched her chest.

Kichi moved to an empty terminal, sat down, and logged on. Her familiar screen, with its wildflower background and country-cottage windows, blossomed onscreen. She checked a few of the latest readings; procogitin and cogitigen levels were going through the roof. "I'm obviously still not as attuned as you people here. How long does it take for the vector to take full effect?"

"Half an hour, maybe more."

"Thanks." Kichi turned to the terminal, and Bev silently stole away, aware without words that she was no longer needed. "Get me Treyl."

Treyl's image was with her at once. "What's the status down there?" he asked. "The people at Site One haven't been very vocal."

"That's not a surprise. The effect seems to be in full swing; they're sensing one another's emotions and responding to what they feel. Bev says that the effect will take a half hour to manifest fully. I imagine that the micro-organisms in my bloodstream are adapting furiously."

"So far, the Project is a success—but only in the small area around Site One. Chance wants you all to be on the lookout for a stable organism that can function without procogitin and cogitigen in the environment."

"Does Chance have any idea how we're supposed to recognize such an organism when we see it?"

Treyl laughed. "Of course not. We have teams in Estremoz watching for its emergence, but it'll show up first where you are." His smile faded. "Once that organism shows up, it's the key to making the Project work off Kaa. It'll have to be isolated from the evolutionary spiral, then brought to Estremoz where it can be cultured and spread."

"You don't ask for much, do you?" The task was daunting, almost hopeless; yet Kichi felt exhilarated, energized. She abruptly realized that they *all* felt that way; there was a job to do, and those here at Site One were the people to do it.

"I know you can do it." Without farewell, Treyl's image faded to nothing.

As Kichi worked, hours passed. Techs were in constant motion, leaving the lab and returning with samples from various parts of the forest; each new sample brought a flurry of activity, a rush to examine the new organisms brought in and to pin down their biochemical behavior. The team worked quickly, wordlessly, with no wasted motions and scant need for words. Just as their terminals were part of a network that linked them together as one, even reaching to Estremoz and Kaa Station, so they themselves were part of a biochemical network that filled the whole lab and sent tendrils forth into the forest.

Kichi felt a presence behind her, turned to see Le approaching. His face was impassive, but just the same she felt his frown. "I've got my people setting up a defense perimeter." He gestured at the lab. "Is this everyone?"

"One or two are out in the field."

"Get them back here. And don't let anyone else leave. I'm going to evac you all to Kaa Station."

She bit her lip. "No."

"What?"

"I said 'no.' It's an expression of refusal or disagreement."

His face didn't move, yet she felt a wave of his anger so tangible that several nearby techs turned their heads. "This is a military camp now, and soon it's going to be a battlefield. I'm not making a request, Kichi."

She took a breath. So easy to respond in anger, to allow the feeling between them to build with each exchange, the way tiny vortices merged into a hurricane.

No. That way wasn't productive. She forced herself to calm down. *Amazing grace, how sweet the sound...* "Le, you've tried your way. Let us try *ours*."

"You *did*. Your way doesn't work either. I'm not going to have another massacre like Birkham on my hands."

"No, you're not," she answered matter-of-factly. "There are half a million natives in the forest around here. You can't make *them* leave...you can't possibly evac them all. So there's no sense in making us leave, not when we're the only hope of avoiding a bloodbath."

A wall of ice sprang up around Le Galvao. "Fine," he said. "*Sidango* is on its way down. Once it arrives, I'm evacking all civilians. With or without your permission. You can bring charges against me when it's all over." He spun smartly and marched out of the lab.

Bev looked up, caught Kichi's eye, and gave a determined nod. All around her, the others echoed the feeling. Until they'd isolated the emergent organism, nothing so simple as the Imperial Marines could get them to leave.

Her terminal beeped, and she punched the answer code. Davad Gomes, another tech from Site One, appeared on her screen. He was obviously standing in the clearing, in front of the Eternity Tree. "Kichi, I think you'd better come out here."

"What's going on?"

"Your friend Darruf is here, along with at least a hundred other natives. And...and She's here too. She's finally arrived. She asked for you."

"Who are you talking about?"

Davad flashed a beatific smile. "Why...King, of course."

*

Finally, after journeying halfway across the world, King has come to the foot of the Eternity Tree. Worldsong has become a swirling tumult, an all-encompassing storm...and here in the clear eye of that storm, the two greatest beings in the world stand one before the other, flesh to bark, while the entire planet holds its breath.

I feel Kichi and the other Humans behind me, and I turn to regard my friend transformed. Always before, Kichi and her folk have seemed dumb, somewhat pitiable creatures; idiot savants who may have conquered the stars, yet can converse only in the manner of children. No matter how often I remind myself that they do not speak and hear the way we do, the impression lingers that they are a bit stupid.

No longer.

Kichi blazes with sensation, with a presence that even a child could read. For the first time, I feel that I can truly know my friend; her moods and her feelings are no longer hidden. It is as if, overnight, a stone statue has come alive. Kichi's soul, which earlier I had only glimpsed in flashes, in pieces as she sang with her voice—Kichi's soul is now fully in place, as fully as any of my own folk.

Kichi, at last, has truly learned to sing.

She feels my surprise, my happiness, and responds with joy of her own. Yet there is also puzzlement, and fear, and awe at the presence of King...and a dreadful sense of urgency, as if something bad is going to happen...and soon.

Before I can pursue that thought, before Kichi and I can move toward one another or even speak—King turns to regard Her children gathered in this sacred place. Then the storm that is Worldsong breaks, and something explodes within my head...and the Miracle begins.

At the dawn of time, the warrior King Ep-Naph brought the gift of consciousness to my folk. What had been dull beasts, dreaming away their unregarded lives in eternal and unknowing sunshine, became a *people*, the conscious expression of Worldsong itself.

I am he, Ep-Naph on the arid plains of Raen, hot sand beneath my feet and the scent of my far-distant people barely a memory in my mind.

I am nameless disciples of Ep-Naph, those of the Brotherhood who preserved his thoughts and his words across decades. Feel the touch of parchment beneath our hands, the rage and scorn of those who in their ignorance drive us away from town and clevth.

I am Dleef, disciple who became King. Stand with me at Ep-Naph's rocky tomb, feel his soul pour forth like water in the desert. Drink deep, submerge in that water, feel it carry you away. Surrender to the current that stirs the world.

I am Dleef, who is also Ep-Naph.

I am Erreaf, daughter of Dleef, King of all the world. Beneath my hands is the dry, rough bark of the Eternity Tree. Around me spins the maelstrom of Worldsong. My soul is the soul of my folk.

I am Erreaf, King, and I am old. I am Dleef, my own father, and I am dying. I am Ep-Naph, alone in the desert, sleeping away the years in the still, silent embrace of death.

I am Darruf of the Clevth of the Westering Hills; Darruf Windtaster, Darruf Riverreader, Darruf Treespeaker. Darruf Touched-By-Fate, Darruf the hands and eyes and antennae of my dying King.

Drink deep, Darruf.

For this, King came into the East. For this, She left Her comfortable home and trekked across half the planet, drove Herself to the edge of death and beyond. She did this of Her own will, which is also the will of the Worldsong.

I am the legacy of Ep-Naph. Bodies come and go, age and die, fall to dust and are forgotten. But I live on.

The bent and withered thing at the base of the Eternity Tree gives up, slumps to the ground. Breath ceases, life departs, and the sweet smell of death begins to spread.

King is dead.

I, alone, am left. I am Darruf Touched-By-Fate. I am Erreaf, I am Dleef, I am Ep-Naph. I am the Brotherhood, I am Worldsong.

I, now, am King. Darruf.

*

From thirty meters above, suspended amid the branches of one of the great trees, Le gave the native ceremony only part of his attention. The rest of his mind was fixed on his detectors, a wide-flung net that would give warning of Jeritza's approach.

There was too much chatter on the comm bands, but Le didn't have the heart to tell his people to shut up. Let them get their nervousness out now, so when the battle came they could focus.

"What's going on down there?"

"Can't you tell? The old King is dying. She's chosen that tall fellow to be her replacement. All her memories are downloading into him." That was de Ornelas, whom the others sometimes called 'Professor.' "It's beautiful."

"De Ornelas, how do *you* know what this is all about?"

"I tell you, I just *know*. It's obvious."

Le shook his head. The natives were an odd bunch, you could never be absolutely sure what they were on about. Even talking to them was a nearly impossible task to anyone but a specialist...and he remembered that even the specialists could only communicate in a primitive kind of pidgin.

Then why wasn't he having any trouble following this ceremony?

Because Kichi's damned Project was actually working?

Le clicked onto *Sidango's* status display. Still half an hour before the ship arrived. He should've told Pavla it was an emergency. He didn't want all these civilians around when Jeritza made his move.

And what about the natives?

Le's lips tightened in a straight line. The natives were bait. Like the labs of Site One. Jeritza *had* to show up. And Le would be ready.

No more massacres. The Butcher's reign ended here and now.

Le was still congratulating himself when the first explosion went off.

*

Major Segm Jeritza, Third Army of the Patalanian Union, was running out of time.

The war had taken its toll on the Union. Trade interdicts, Imperial raids on shipping, the war effort itself...all had brought shortages to the Union. Food wasn't the problem, most planets were self-sufficient in food. But manufactured goods, raw materials, cybernetics and medical technology, pharmaceuticals: there the Union was hurting.

Particularly pharmaceuticals.

Jeritza had done his best. Sixty-three planets, every one of them a key supplier, brought over to the Union—a career total that no other Patalanian officer could match. Jeritza went in when the Union needed quick results, and he always delivered the goods. He was most persuasive. In the life-or-death struggle with the Empire, Segm Jeritza did not hesitate to use both life and death as weapons.

Kaa was a special case.

Possessed of the strangest biochemistry in the Galaxy, Kaa was the source of over half of the Union's drugs...and the *only* source for drugs to combat the Hlekkarian Plague and a dozen other, more minor, maladies. So far, the Kaa Cartel had swayed in a well-balanced neutrality, dealing with black markets on both sides. The President and the Generals who directed the Union's war effort had been content to let Kaa stay neutral.

Then, eventually, Kaa's strategic nature penetrated to the slow-witted Imperials. The Empire had many sources for drugs: the Union had only one. Take control of Kaa, cut off the black-market traffic to the Union, and in two years Patala would be so wracked by plague that the war would end.

The Empire started to move toward Kaa. And the Kaa Cartel, damn their eyes, seemed content to go along. The flood of drugs from Kaa became a trickle, then stopped altogether.

So the Generals sent Jeritza.

And now, Jeritza was running out of time. The 307th was on-planet, Imperial reinforcements on their way. And at home, his two teenage daughters lay in a coma, waiting for the free flow of drugs to resume.

There was no time for delicacy, no time for persuasion, no time to be subtle. The only tactic left was the one that had served him so well in the past: hit them. Hit them hard, make them know they were hurt. Give them no choice.

He'd been stupid the first time, thinking that the Humans controlled Kaa's destiny. Distracted by Le Galvao and his troop of clowns. But it wasn't the Humans at all who were important. With enough provocation, the Humans would leave Kaa altogether.

No, it was the natives who were the rulers here. The natives who needed to be hit. Just enough to let them know Jeritza meant business.

His lips tightened. The charges were set, his people knew what to do. It merely remained for him to give the order.

And if, in the process of securing Kaa, Le Galvao had to be eliminated...so much the better.

*

Kichi couldn't help but scream when half the grove went up in flame.

Shock, fear, pain—all raced around her and through her, waves of feeling one after another. She heard her own scream echoed by Humans and natives alike, felt panic building in her guts. Without thinking, she turned, started to run...then panic faded and something stopped her.

Le's people, in mirror-surfaced battle gear, floated down from the treetops: a dozen silvery statues, monuments to bravery and justice, cavalry come to the rescue. The air was suddenly full of bright laser bolts.

Across the glade, ten meters away at the foot of the Eternity Tree, Darruf looked up and met her eyes. He raised himself up on his hindmost limbs, and all the natives around him followed suit.

(Little Ones, your time has come. For this you were brought here.)

Slowly, Kichi moved forward, oblivious to fire and soldiers and intervening bodies of whatever species. She heard Darruf, heard him not in the pidgin that she ordinarily used but in his own language, rich and wonderful.

He sang.

"Here we meet, my good and gracious friend. Darruf and Kichi. Kaanese and Human. Here we join in the rich melodies of Worldsong. I welcome you."

Beside her, not three meters away, a man died: his defense screen overloaded and he perished in a flash of heat and light, sending his dying pain out in an expanding wave that swept through Kichi with the sensation of a million hot knives. She shivered, stumbled, then it was over.

Darruf winced, then gave her his hand.

"Together we are and together our folk will remain. Melody and counterpoint. We provide the song, you the words. Between us, meaning emerges."

Kichi gestured at the fiery chaos around them. "We've got to stop this."

"Worldsong agrees. Sing with us."

Kichi turned to face carnage. Three dead bodies, no, four. A soldier cradled a burnt arm; Kichi felt the pain in her own limb. Natives and Humans were scrambling for cover, cowering behind tree trunks and rocks, or just running as fast as they could.

Motionless, mirror-surfaced, Le Galvao stood in the center. Then...a motion of his hand, like a conductor leading an orchestra, and the sky changed.

Blue sky and cloud were replaced by green trees and ground, a mirrored hemisphere a quarter-kilometer across, centered on the grove. Defense screens, Kichi thought. He *was* ready for Jeritza. And now he's barricaded us all in together.

For a moment she had a wild vision, of laser cannon perched outside the screen, ready to pour megajoules of energy into the grove, to incinerate every living thing. Is that why he wanted us gone?

As if he'd read her thought—and perhaps he *had*—Le turned to her and shook his head. No, of course he wouldn't destroy everything. He needed to make sure that Jeritza was dead. He needed to see the body, to kill the man with his own hands.

"Le, there's no need for that." No need. With her heightened perceptions, between Worldsong and Darruf and the quiet music of the Eternity Tree under the surface of her mind, she knew that the Project was a success. She could *feel* it. In the heady biochemical brew of the grove, under run-away evolution gone mad and natural selection directed by the Hlutr, the emergent organism had come into being, was reproducing and spreading. It no longer needed the presence of the natives.

Let Jeritza hide, let him run. He was undoubtedly infected, he would only carry the organism with him to every world he touched. Feeling every sensation of his victims, his own body echoing their pain, unable to tune it out or turn it off...Jeritza would never kill again.

Le shook his head again, then jumped toward the treetops with antigrav grace, leaving behind only his icy determination.

"Darruf, we have to do something. We have to stop him."

"Sing with us, Kichi Wemes."

A preternatural stillness fell over the grove, and Kichi was suddenly conscious of those who surrounded her. Natives, Darruf's followers; Humans, from the lab; the Chorus of the Wood. They were all silent, as silent as the forest itself, as silent as the departed Le. Even Worldsong, on the fringes of her consciousness, was muted.

She took a breath, and sang.

Where are your eyes that looked so mild, huroo, huroo...?

*

Le cornered Jeritza against the eastern edge of the defense screen. The Patalanian had his people digging, as if he thought that Le would have forgotten to extend the screen belowground. They'd already dug a sizable hole, deep enough that Le couldn't easily see the diggers inside. Jeritza stood a few meters from the excavation, wearing Patalanian battle armor and a Major's insignia on his helmet.

Le waited for a second, wondering if it could be this easy. Just toss a grenade, grav warp, that would be it. They'd never find even a trace of Jeritza. Of course, the implosion would kill Le as well, but he'd been prepared to pay *that* price for quite a while.

He reached for his belt, then froze. His eyes narrowed, and he upped the magnification on his goggles. What was it?

Jeritza stood with his back to Le. And no one was on watch. Almost as if inviting an attack.

What if it *wasn't* Jeritza?

Then Le would die for nothing. And the Butcher of Theras Five would once again escape.

Suppose it *was* Jeritza, and Le didn't attack?

He had to know.

He eased his laser rifle out of its harness, took careful aim…
and fired over the figure's shoulder, only a centimeter to the
left of its head. Defense screen flared, reflecting the beam, then
vanishing.

The other didn't turn. But return fire came from the pit, and
Le jumped backwards, behind a tree.

That wasn't Jeritza. It probably wasn't even human, just an
inflatable dummy or a corpse dressed up. The troops in the pit
might not be real either, just automatic weapons.

Then where in space was Jeritza?

Le swallowed hard. Where he could take hostages. Where
he could deal with the natives. The grove.

Kichi!

Heedless of the weapons at his back, Le jumped.

*

Kichi and Darruf still touched, soft Human hand against
rough Kaanese exoskeleton. At least, she thought, Jeritza had
left them *that* when he captured them.

"Can't you feel what I feel, Jeritza?" she called out to the
hulking giant in Patalanian battle gear. She held up Darruf's
hand. "You *do* feel it, don't you? Every sensation. Every little
movement." She laughed. "You can't kill us, any of us. You
couldn't take the pain. You'd kill yourself."

His patronizing smile belied the worry he was casting forth
into Worldsong. "A soldier learns to endure pain. But you're
right about one thing: at least I *will* have to kill you quickly.
Don't worry, I'm very familiar with the techniques. Or, at least,
the theory." He glanced to the right, where one of his
lieutenants stood with a display screen. "Where's Galvao?"

"Don' know yet."

"Find him."

Maybe Jeritza knew what he was talking about. His people
had arrived carrying corpses, members of the 307th now

heaped in a pile before the lab. He'd managed to kill *them*, hadn't he?

But how many of his own people had died in the attempt? So far as Kichi could tell, there were only the two with him, the man with the display screen and a woman guarding the hostages.

Damn it, she didn't know enough about how the Project worked. What variations were there from person to person? How possible was it, that Jeritza might escape the full effect?

Darruf's hand moved in hers. Across the silent song between them came a message: "This shall pass, my friend. The Human is bluffing. He does not intend to kill us. He cannot."

Thank you, Darruf. Now if I could only persuade myself to trust your ability to decode unfamiliar Human emotions.

"Let them go, Jeritza." Le's voice, unamplified, echoed in the stillness of the grove.

Jeritza turned and smiled at the Imperial officer. "Captain Galvao. A pleasure to meet face-to-face at last. I assume you have come to offer me your surrender?"

"Not bloody likely. I'm here to fight you."

Kichi swore. "Le, don't do this."

"Shut up, Kichi. This won't take a moment."

"I hope not," Jeritza replied, then leapt.

The man was a demon, moving far more quickly than any Human had a right to move. Le's laser beam cut through empty space; Jeritza, three meters to the right, fired and caught Le directly in the chest. Le's defense screen flared, and all Kichi felt was a slight warmth on her bosom.

"They're going to kill each other. Help me, Darruf."

"Together, my friend. Together."

She joined hands with Darruf, reached for the swirling melody of Worldsong. For an instant, disbelief stopped her— chemicals, it's all chemicals, there's no song and no way to stop this. Then she found Worldsong, and Darruf was with her, Darruf and all his people, half a million strong in the forest around.

She groped for words, made do with a simple yet fervent wish: Stop the fighting.

Jeritza leapt at Le, and sparks flew.

*

Le Galvao remembered the jungles of Theras Five.

Jeritza leapt past him, swung a truncheon—and Le's defense screen went down in a shower of sparks. But Le kept his senses, jerked right, and caught Jeritza in the shoulder. Momentum interrupted, the Patalanian went down.

Le felt him hit the ground, felt it in his bones and flesh.

A defense screen stopped electromagnetic beams, and any projectiles with sufficient energy. It was agony reaching through Jeritza's field—agony that momentarily paralyzed Jeritza. Ha, thought Le, you weren't expecting that! He grabbed a pistol from his belt, swung it, and hit Jeritza's power supply. He felt the casing break. A moment later, the defense screen went down.

Hand-to-hand, then, Le thought. He kicked, felt his own breath go out of his body as his foot connected. Every blow, every shock, every contact—he and Jeritza would share them all. As would all the onlookers.

He felt a wide grin. Sorry, Kichi, I didn't mean for you to be part of this.

Jeritza swung something—a spanner?—and caught Le on the right temple. Stars spun, his head split, and Le fell backwards on the ground.

"Stop it!" Kichi screamed. "You don't have any choice."

Le swam in a red haze. The jungle. Theras Five. Birkham. Headless, armless bodies. Gutted survivors begging for death. The stench of mud and shit and blood.

He had his hands around Jeritza's throat, pressed his fingers into the yielding flesh, felt them around his own throat. "This is it, you bastard," he grunted. "Now you pay."

"Le!" Kichi's voice was choked, her hand on his arm barely even there. "For gods' sakes, stop it. It's over."

"No. Nev-er o-ver." Never.

In the back of his mind, Le heard the opening bars of the Imperial Anthem. Somewhere else, he felt a gash in his gut, felt something moving in his vitals, something that didn't belong. Red and black fought for his vision.

"Damn you, both of you! *You're killing us.* You're killing yourselves. Is it *that* important to you, that you hate? Is it more important to hate than to live?"

Le tried to explain to her, tried to tell her about honor and justice, about the Empire and what it stood for. But he couldn't speak, couldn't keep his thoughts on track. He was sick, he retched blood and that didn't help.

Theras Five.

Birkham.

Die, condemn you! Die!

The Anthem. He'd always loved it, ever since he was a boy....

She's right, you know. It's the hate, more than anything else. Jeritza says it's glory and honor and the needs of the Union, I say it's duty and justice and the Empire, and all along it's all so much bluster, frightened little boys defending their turf.

Something took his finger and twisted, kept twisting until the bones cracked—and didn't stop even then.

It hurts. Shit, it hurts, I never knew it would hurt like this.

He coughed, gasped, fell to his knees. His fingers were numb, he didn't even know if they were still around Jeritza's throat. He couldn't through the haze of darkness.

Kichi's right, we have to stop, there's no sense to this.

He tried to rise, slipped, and fell.

With his last bit of strength, Le willed his fingers to close tighter around whatever they held.

So the only things left were hate and pain. And the pain, he couldn't even call his own.

At least he owned his hate....

*

With your guns and drums and drums and guns, huroo, huroo
With your guns and drums and drums and guns, huroo, huroo
With your guns and drums and drums and guns
The enemy nearly slew ye
Oh my darling dear, you look so queer
And Johnny, I hardly knew ye.

*

The Kaa Cartel stood around Le's grave, translucent images against the green of the Wood. They waited patiently while Kichi and the others finished their song; then Sayyid Alma deVigny lifted her hands in benediction.

"Captain Galvao was a true hero of the Empire. His monument will be raised among those of the other heroes on Laxus; but his body will remain here on Kaa, where he was born and where he achieved his greatest triumph."

There was little applause, either from the Humans or the natives. The crowd waited for a few moments, then began to disperse in twos and threes.

The other members of the Cartel faded away, leaving only Treyl behind. He stood at attention until Kichi and Darruf approached him.

"Thank you for coming, Treyl," Kichi said. "The symbolism means a lot to everyone."

"But it's only a symbol, isn't it? Whatever Kaa is becoming, I feel that the Cartel is increasingly irrelevant to it."

Kichi nodded. "Darruf says that we are all part of the Legacy of Ep-Naph. He wants you to know that you'll always be welcome at the King's Court."

Treyl smiled. "Thank you. The symbolism means a lot."

Kichi shrugged. "You should be happy. The Project worked. You have the organism to spread through the whole sector. Maybe Sayyid Alma's right, and you can prevent some future wars.

"I'm happy. We all are. Extending the Project beyond Kaa is going to keep all of us busy and happy for the rest of our lives. And we'll know that we've made a contribution to the Galaxy."

The sun broke through cloud, brightening the grove. Kichi cocked her head at Treyl, frowned. "Then what is it? I can't read you, Treyl."

He took a breath. "The Cartel voted this morning not to take advantage of the Project. The organism won't be released in the general population. There's still too much we don't know. We're all set in our ways. We're going to stay up here in the Station, and deal with the rest of the Galaxy. You'll go your own way, without our interference."

"Then why so sad?"

"Like you said, I'm happy." He looked off into the distance. "I'm about as happy as I can stand, as happy as I'll ever be. I have no right to complain. But you, Kichi…you and Darruf and everyone else on Kaa—you're something different now. You know feelings in a way that I can't. I have happiness, but you know Joy. And I can't help but wonder what it feels like…."

Treyl's image faded, and Darruf gave Kichi one of his hands. "Come, my friend. We have much to do." Together, they strode out of the sight of the Eternity Tree.

Around them, Worldsong's silent melodies spun on.

*

So ends the First Book of Darruf, King. And so continues the Legacy of Ep-Naph….

TIMELINE

2153 CE Terran Empire founded.
TE 203 Kaa discovered.
TE 204 Kaa Cartel organized to control trade in pharmaceuticals and to protect natives.
TE 224 Human settlement Estremoz founded.
c. TE 300 Ep-Naph dies.
TE 304 Patalanian Union secedes from Empire; Patalanian War begins.
TE 361 Battle of Karphos. Patalanian Union begins expansion throughout the Transgeled.
TE 378 Leristec Treyl born.
TE 379 Dleef born.
TE 403 *A Voice in Every Wind*.
TE 418 Le Galvao, Kichi Wemes born.
TE 443 Patalanian forces capture Kaa. Cartel agrees to neutrality in trade, in exchange for nominal independence.
TE 455 Battle of Teras Five.
TE 464 INS *Sidango* arrives to re-establish Imperial presence on Kaa. *Marching Home Again*.

CHRONOLOGICAL SEQUENCE

These stories are part of a broader universe that spans nearly three billion years of history and hundreds of thousands of worlds. Other books and stories set in this universe have been, and will continue to be, written and published out of sequence. The Chrolonological Sequence system, like the Dewey Decimal System of library fame, assigns numbers to eras and events rather than dates, and allows new works to be fit between existing ones. For more information, visit the Scattered Worlds website at *www.scatteredworlds.com*.

The Chronological Sequence numbers for the stories in this book are:

4.882: "A Voice in Every Wind"
4.982: "Marching Home Again"

Scattered Worlds Chronology

0.0 (before 2.4 billion BCE) - PRE-PYLISTROPH; Sapient life in the Gathered Worlds

1.0 (c. 2.4 billion BCE) - THE PYLISTROPH; Seed Vessels launched

2.0 (c. 1.2 billion BCE) - GERGATHAN PROCLAIMS MERTORTHAR Flight of the Daamin; Schism of the Hlutr; Empires of the Scattered Worlds

3.0 (c. 100,000 BCE) - PRE-IMPERIAL TERRA
3.75 (2042 CE) - *Dance for the Ivory Madonna*
3.85 (20698 CE) - *Hunt for the Dymalon Cygnet*
3.962 (2103 CE) - "Gamester"
3.968 (2103 CE) - "Big Improvement"

4.0 (2153 CE/TE 0) - FIRST TERRAN EMPIRE
4.55 (TE 219) - *Weaving the Web of Days*
4.74 (TE 321) - *The Eighth Succession*
4.75 (TE 335) - *Children of the Eighth Day*
4.852 (TE k361) - "Candelabra and Diamonds"
4.882 (TE 403) - "A Voice in Every Wind"
4.982 (TE 463) - "Marching Home Again"

5.0 (2624 CE) - INTERREGNUM
5.38 (6484 CE) - *A Rose From Old Terra*

6.0 (2488 CE/12,488 HE) - FEDERATION OF FAMILIES
6.55 (c. 17,700 HE) "The Geas Ingenerate"

7.0 (20,724 HE) - SECOND TERRAN EMPIRE

8.0 (24,356 HE) - POST-IMPERIAL HUMANITY
8.5 (c. 30,000 HE) - *The Leaves of October*

9.0 (c. 3 million HE) - ENDTIME

The Milky Way Galaxy
TE 464

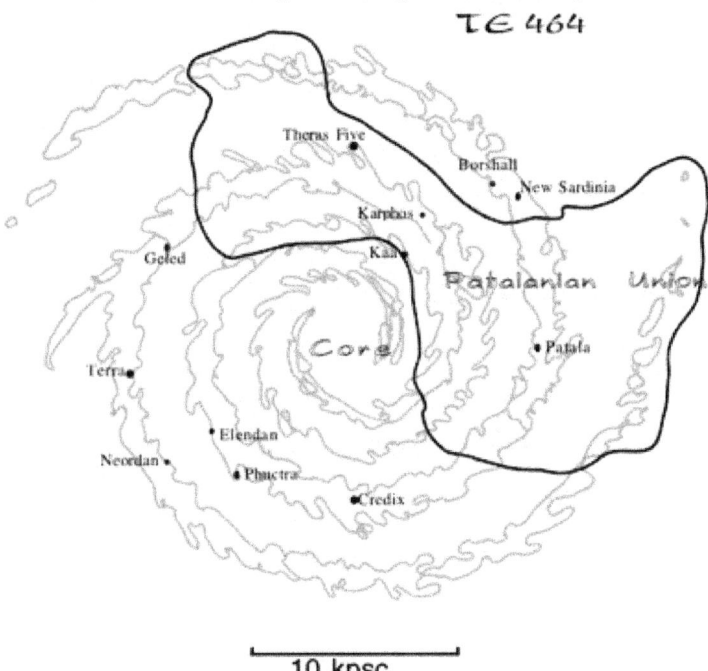

10 kpsc

The Scattered Worlds Mosaic by Don Sakers

Dance for the Ivory Madonna
a romance of psiberspace
Print & Kindle
Spectrum Award finalist; 56 Hugo nominations
"Imagine a Stand on Zanzibar written by a left-wing Robert Heinlein, and infused with the most exciting possibilities of the new cyber-technology." -Melissa Scott, author of Dreaming Metal, The Jazz

Weaving the Web of Days
a tale of the Scattered Worlds
Print & Kindle
Maj Thovold has led the Galaxy for three decades, a Golden Age of peace and prosperity. She is weary and ready to resign, but she faces one last battle: a battle on the strangest battlefield known: a web of living tendrils that stretches across interstellar space. A web where Maj's enemies wait, like spiders, for their prey....

The Eighth Succession
a novel of the Scattered Worlds
Print & Kindle
"Remember when science fiction used to be filled with galactic intrigue and bigger-than-life heroes? The wonderful Don Sakers certainly does! The Eighth Succession is a rip-roaring yarn, impossible to put down. If John W. Campbell's Astounding Stories had been published in an LGBT-friendly era, this is the cover-story serial you'd have been waiting anxiously for each month. What a ride!" -Robert J. Sawyer, Hugo Award-winning author of Red Planet Blues

Children of the Eighth Day
a novel of the Scattered Worlds
Print & Kindle
The Eighth Succession *introduced readers to the Hoister Family...* Children of the Eighth Day *takes the story of this remarkable family to the exciting next level.*

The Scattered Worlds Mosaic by Don Sakers

All Roads Lead to Terra
two tales of the Scattered Worlds
Kindle only
Two exciting tales tell of attacks against the shining jewel of the Terran Empire: Earth. Includes an introduction and notes from the author.

A Voice in Every Wind
two tales of the Scattered Worlds
Print & Kindle
On a world where meaning lives in every rock and stream, and every breeze brings a new voice, one human explorer stands on the threshold of discoveries that could alter the future of Humanity.

A Rose From Old Terra
a novel of the Scattered Worlds
Print & Kindle
Jedrek left the Grand Library and his work circle eleven years ago. Now a crisis in uncharted space brings the circle back together. Soon, Jedrek and his friends are at the focal point of a clash of cultures, and the only thing that can save the Galaxy is one modest group of Librarians.

The Leaves of October
a novel of the Scattered Worlds
Print & Kindle
Compton Crook Award finalist
The Hlutr: Immensely old, terribly wise…and utterly alien. When mankind went out into the stars, he found the Hlutr waiting for him. Waiting to observe, to converse, to help. Waiting to judge…and, if necessary, to destroy.

More Books from Speed-of-C Productions

The Curse of the Zwilling by Don Sakers
Print & Kindle

It's Hogwarts meets Buffy at Patapsco University: a small, cozy liberal arts college like so many others – except for the Department of Comparative Religion, where age-old spells are taught and magic is practiced. When a favorite teacher is found dead under mysterious circumstances, grad student David Galvin finds that a malevolent evil has awakened. And now David, along with four novice undergrads, must defeat this ancient, malignant terror.

The SF Book of Days by Don Sakers
Print only

Drawn from the pages of classic sf literature, here is a science fiction/fantasy event for every day of the year…and for quite a few days that aren't part of the year. From Doc Brown's arrival in Hill Valley (January 1, 1885) to the launch of the Bellerophon (Sextor 7, 2351), this datebook is truly out of this world.

PsiScouts #1: At Risk by Don Sakers & Phil Meade
Print & Kindle

In the 26th century, psi-powered teenagers from all over the Myriad Worlds join together as the heroic PsiScouts.

PsiScouts #2: Bright Promise by Don Sakers & Phil Meade
Print & Kindle

Further adventures of the heroic PsiScouts in the 26th century.

Meat and Machine: queer writings by Don Sakers
Print & Kindle

Don Sakers has been queering sf and fantasy for three decades. Meat and Machine collects 24 short pieces of Don's science fiction, fantasy, nonfiction, and erotics.

Elevenses by Don Sakers
Print & Kindle

Eleven SF and fantasy short stories intended as bite-size snacks.

More Books from Speed-of-C Productions

Gaylaxicon Sampler 2006
Print only
Sample the work of thirteen writers from across the spectrum of gay, lesbian, bisexual, and/or transgender science fiction, fantasy, and/or horror. Includes big names and small, much-published veterans and promising beginners, Lammy and Spectrum Award nominees and winners, past Gaylaxicon Guests of Honor, and fresh new names.

QSpec Sampler 2007
Print only
Originally prepared as a giveaway at Gaylaxicon 2007 in Atlanta, this volume is available at a nominal charge as a sampler of the fine work being done by GLBT writers in SF, fantasy, and horror.

Lucky in Love by Don Sakers
Print & Kindle
When his best friend Keith moved away, there was a big hole left in Frank's life. Then a bad car crash put him in the hospital. While there recovering, he got a visit from the star of his high school basketball team, Purnell Johnson. It wasn't long before his luck started to improve.

Five Planes by Melissa Scott & Don Sakers
Print & Kindle
Space opera adventure. Pirates. Judges. Weird physics. Desperate refugees. Struggling colonists. Missing persons and a mystery ship. A quest for human origins in a pocket universe.

A Cosmos of Many Mansions: Varieties of SF by Don Sakers
Print & Kindle
Based on the first five years of Sakers's popular review column, this volume examines & explains dozens of types of science fiction along with hundreds of reviews.

The Mud of the Place by Susanna J. Sturgis
Print only
"A sensitive, witty, and tightly plotted portrayal of life on Martha's Vineyard that only a true Islander could have written. Nice going, Susanna!" –Cynthia Riggs

www.ingramcontent.com/pod-product-compliance
Lightning Source LLC
Chambersburg PA
CBHW070636130626
46555CB00006B/2575